## TRIPLE PLAY!

It was the top of the ninth. The Sox had just pulled ahead of the Dodgers with one run.

"No sweat! We got the lead!" cried Scrapper as he ran out to take his position at second. "Let's hold 'em!"

After a tough game, the Sox pitcher was tired and the first two Dodger batters got on base with clean singles.

When the third batter, a left-hander, stepped up to the plate, Scraps motioned for the first baseman to cover the infield hole while he moved closer to the shortstop.

Fouling off the first two pitches, the batter connected with the third in a line drive directly toward second. Scrapper didn't hesitate. He gloved it backhanded, spun around to touch second, doubling out the runner already on his way to third, then fired to first to end the game with another win for the Sox.

Other books in the ROOKIES series:

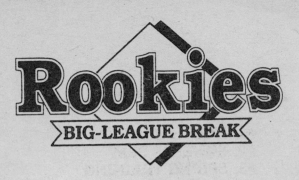

# Rookies
## BIG-LEAGUE BREAK

**Mark Freeman**

BALLANTINE BOOKS • NEW YORK

RLI: <u>VL: 6 & up</u>
IL: 6 & up

Library of Congress Catalog Card Number: 89-91173

ISBN 0-345-35905-4

Manufactured in the United States of America

First Edition: August 1989
Third Edition: April 1990

To Kelly Caudell

Special thanks to Marian Caudell.

# ONE

Roberto "Magic" Ramirez was psyched for the game with the league-leading Tucson Astros.

He sat on the edge of the bench in the Albuquerque Dodger dugout while his team batted in the top of the first. Behind him, he could hear the fans roar as second baseman, Dennis Packard, hit a hard line drive through the middle.

Roberto felt like cheering, too, not just for the hit against the favored team, but for his own good luck. After a spectacular year in the Salem Dodgers, he had proven himself in spring training enough to get promoted to AAA ball, just one step below the majors. If his luck held, he could be in Los Angeles next year.

When Greg Stuart, the next batter, struck out, it didn't get his spirits down. Neither did Cary's fly ball to right field nor Willy's ground-out to third base.

As the Astros ran in from the field and the

Dodgers ran out, Roberto walked to the mound. He took a few minutes to stretch out his arms and glance up into the stands. He liked Albuquerque. He liked the warm, sometimes hot, days and the cool evenings. But most of all he liked the bigger stadium and the larger, noisier crowds.

It was early in the season but already Roberto was earning a reputation. He had three wins to his credit and had allowed a total of only eight balls in the outfield. Five were fly balls. His ERA was 1.20. Magic was on a roll.

He flexed his knees as the first batter stepped to the plate. Then he delivered his split-fingered fastball for a call strike. His second pitch was high and inside, forcing the batter to lean away from it. Two quick curves sent the man back to the dugout, shaking his head as he went.

The Astros' second batter grounded out to the shortstop and the third popped up to shallow right field on an outside pitch.

Roberto left the mound, put on his jacket, and leaned back against the wall of the dugout while his teammates went down in batting order. The Astros had a good pitcher, too, but Roberto wasn't worried. There were eight innings to go and he had as much confidence in the Dodger team as he had in himself.

The first man he faced in the top of the second was Astro power hitter, Lefty Williams. Roberto wanted to keep the ball chest high and not give him a chance to get under it. Lefty, overanxious, swung at the first pitch and fouled it back into the stands. He fouled two more before Roberto's curve ball caught him off guard and he sent a short chopper to the second baseman for an easy out.

Billy Mills stepped up. Coach's pregame reminders of the opposing team's batting habits had included Billy's tendency to crowd the plate. Roberto squinted and leaned forward slightly, studying the narrowed strike zone as the player dug in. He would have to pitch him tight and keep the ball away from the outside. Billy was also known to jump on outside pitches. Roberto was determined not to give him that chance.

Winding up, he whipped a fastball straight past the top of Billy's knees for an oh-and-ond count. The fans cheered as catcher Jim Graves threw the ball back to Roberto, squatted down, and gave his pitcher the signal for an inside curve.

With a slight nod of his head, Roberto fired the ball in so close that Billy had to suck in his stomach. As he did so, his bat came around almost halfway but he checked the swing before he broke his wrists and the ump called it a ball.

Astro fans booed the near miss but Dodger fans were ecstatic, some of them chanting, "Strikeout! Strikeout!"

Roberto thought that after that last pitch Billy would move back from the plate a little, but he didn't. He dug in deeper and held his ground.

Aware that a sidearm curve ball looks like it's coming right at you, Roberto decided to make that his next pitch, hoping Billy wouldn't react quick enough to check his swing even if the pitch wasn't in the strike zone.

Standing sideways on the mound and studying the batter, Roberto paused before he began his windup. At the plate, Billy crouched slightly, his bat making tiny circles above his right shoulder as he waited for the next pitch.

Roberto began his windup. And then it happened.

The ball, with all of Roberto's power behind it, slid off the tips of his fingers, spinning in a deadly arc straight for Billy's head. Mills saw it coming but he couldn't react quick enough. It crashed into the side of his head, knocking his batting helmet off. Billy crumpled under the blow and lay in the dust.

Horrified, Roberto ran from the mound toward the fallen batter but was quickly pushed aside by the Astro coach and fellow players, who raced from the dugout and clustered around Billy. Roberto tried to get a look over their shoulders but all he could see was Billy's lifeless, outstretched legs.

When he heard a terse, "Get a stretcher!" his heart began to hammer hard. The pounding noise in his ears sounded deafening in a stadium that had suddenly gone silent.

"Maybe we shouldn't move him," said one of Billy's teammates.

"We've got to get him to a hospital," said another.

"Move back," ordered Billy's coach, "and let the doc through."

Roberto stepped back with the rest. Some of the opposing players noticed him. One opened his mouth as if to say something and then quickly shut it. Roberto's stricken expression was proof that it had been an accident.

After a quick examination by Dr. Benson, Billy's coach and trainer carefully lifted him onto the stretcher and started off the field with the still-unconscious player. It was then that Roberto saw the blood seeping from Billy's left ear.

Instead of returning to the mound, he stood there and watched as Billy was carried into the clubhouse. He didn't even see Ben Davis, his pitching coach, standing beside him.

"You okay, Ramirez?"

Without looking directly at Davis, Roberto nodded but when he got back to the mound and saw another batter at the plate, he knew he wasn't.

His first pitch was high and outside for ball one. The next two were also outside. His fourth was so far from the plate that it sped by the catcher, who had to chase it down, sending the batter to first on a walk.

Roberto took off his cap and ran the back of his hand over his forehead, resettled the cap, and waited for the throw back from his catcher.

But instead of throwing the ball back, Jim Graves walked to the mound. He had played in the minors longer than Roberto and had caught too many pitchers not to recognize that something was wrong.

Dodger manager Cap Capella saw the signs, too, and hurried out to join them. With him came Bobby Parsons, who had been warming up in the bullpen.

"Take a breather, Ramirez," ordered Capella. "You're letting that hit batter get to you. We'll talk about it later."

Roberto went to the dugout, threw his glove down, and sat on the bench, resting his head in his hands.

"Tough break, Magic," said one of the other pitchers. "I remember the first time I beaned a batter. Really shook me up. But I got over it. So will you." Then, as an afterthought, he added, "Best thing to do is get right back in there."

Roberto nodded but he wondered if he could ever "get right back in there." He had played a lot of baseball and had seen a lot of batters get hit, but he had never seen one get knocked out. And bleeding from the ear could mean a serious head injury.

As he thought about that possibility, his natural moodiness hit a new low. He forced himself to face the playing field and try to follow the game, but his mind was on Billy Mills.

He wasn't even aware that the game was over until he heard shouts of "Way to go!" and "Ya-hoo!" as his teammates ran in from the field.

Still upset, Roberto followed the others into the locker room where everyone was talking at once.

"Four to zip!"

"We clobbered 'em!" One player slammed his fist into a locker door and growled.

"Hey, you dink! That's my locker you're hitting!"

"How 'bout those 'league-leading' Astros!"

"Piece o' cake!"

"Yeah."

"No 'All-You-Can-Eat' joints tonight! This calls for a celebration. Anyone for Alfredo's?"

The question was answered by a chorus of "Right ons".

No one seemed to notice Roberto's silence or lack of enthusiasm. They were too caught up in the victory. While they joked and bantered with each other, Roberto showered, got dressed, and quietly left the locker room.

No one saw him leave, either—no one except

Johnny Wiggins, and he wouldn't have stopped him even if he could. The rest were having too much fun talking about the game. The Astros had been expected to sweep the three-game series.

Shouts of "One down, two to go!" echoed from the walls.

Only when Capella appeared and yelled, "Ramirez!" did they settle down.

When Roberto failed to come forward, Capella asked, "Where's Ramirez?"

The players looked at each other and shrugged their shoulders.

"Maybe he's still in the shower," suggested one. "Hey, Magic!" he yelled in the direction of the stalls.

When no one answered, Capella looked at Roberto's roommate. "Graves? Any ideas?"

Jim Graves, a good-natured, five-year veteran with sandy hair, shook his head. "He was here a few minutes ago, Cap. Maybe he went back onto the field. Might have left his glove outside. I'll check." Jim jumped up and headed for the door.

"Save your strength," said Johnny. "The kid left." At thirty-five, he was the oldest and most experienced man on the team. He'd made the round trip from Albuquerque to Los Angeles and back again, playing good solid ball for the parent team but never quite making it to superstar status. After a series of minor injuries, he lost his starting position in L.A. to a rookie. But he wasn't bitter about it. He understood the game just as he understood that Roberto needed to be alone for awhile.

"Left?" Capella couldn't believe his ears. "I told him I wanted to talk to him."

Jim, who knew Roberto better than anyone else on the team, looked down at the floor and mumbled, "He was pretty shook-up over hitting Mills. I guess he just wanted to be by himself. He's like that sometimes."

"I'm not in a very good mood myself," said Capella. "Tell him I want to see him first thing in the morning. And I mean early."

"Sure."

"He'll probably show up at Alfredo's," said Cary Woolston, the Dodger right fielder. "We can all tell him. He's probably there right now, getting a head start on us."

"Yeah. Don't sweat it, Cap," added Dennis.

"It's Ramirez who'll be sweating, not me." Cap, scowling, stalked from the room.

Jim didn't say anything to the others, but he knew Roberto wouldn't be at Alfredo's. He just hoped the rookie was okay. Walking out on the manager could mean big trouble.


Roberto headed in the general direction of the motel where he and Jim shared a room, but when he got there he couldn't remember any of the streets he had taken.

Once inside the room, he stretched out on his bed, clasped his hands under his head, and stared at the ceiling. All he could see was Billy's helmet flying and Billy being carried away. He had hit a player in a high school game once—a glancing blow off the boy's foot. But it hadn't knocked him out. The boy had trotted down to first without even a limp. Even so, his luck had changed after that and it had taken him three games of erratic pitching before he got back into top form.

He wasn't feeling sorry for himself. He was thinking about Billy Mills, worrying about how seriously he was injured and if he, Roberto, had ended the boy's career with that one wild pitch.

He finally fell asleep fully dressed, and didn't even hear Jim come in several hours later.

Not wanting to wake his friend, Jim fumbled around in the darkened room lit only by the light from the parking lot, found a piece of motel notepaper, and scribbled, "R.— See Cap first thing tomorrow." Then he laid the note on the edge of the dresser and dropped exhausted into the bed across from Roberto.

Sometime before dawn Roberto began to dream. He was on the mound, throwing his split-fingered fastball. Batter after batter stepped up to the plate and one after another Roberto knocked them down. He wanted to stop pitching but couldn't. Jim kept throwing the ball back to him and giving him the same signal over and over.

He awoke with a gasp. Sitting straight up he looked around the room, not recognizing it at first. Then he saw Jim sound asleep. Making as little noise as possible, he put on his jacket and opened the door.

When he closed it, Jim's note, caught by a draft of air, fluttered to the floor and lodged under the dresser.

# TWO

Glen "Scrapper" Mitchell clenched and un-
clenched his hands in the locker room. He kept
asking himself: Why?—why was he sent to Vancouver to play AAA ball when he was as good as
or better than most of the major league second
basemen right now? He'd shown that he had what
it took at spring training, so why didn't he get sent
immediately to the Chicago team?

"You listening, Mitchell?" Charlie Cravens, the
Vancouver manager, barked.

"Yeah, yeah, sure," answered Scrapper in a tone
that made his team members throw sidelong
glances in his direction. They were sitting in the
locker room as Cravens went over stats from the
previous season.

"I don't have to remind anyone, even our three
new members, that we finished in the cellar."
There were a few loan moans before Cravens
continued. "That's not going to happen again.

We're going to work—and work hard—on offense *and* defense. And use every ounce of strategy we can come up with."

*Strategy*, thought Scrapper. *I was raised on strategy.*

Sitting up straighter, he crossed his arms and studied the other players. Most were veterans of at least two or three years, some longer. The only newcomers, besides himself, were a promising young pitcher, Jay Deckard, and Ray Hargis, Vancouver's center fielder and Scrapper's roommate.

"All right," said Cravens, "here's the line-up and batting order for tomorrow night: Garrison, shortstop; Fuller, first base; Hargis, center field; Oliver, right field; Brown, catcher . . ."

Scrapper, flushing with anger at not leading off, listened for his name.

Cravens's voice droned on, ". . . Perez, third; Hotchkiss, left; Mitchell, . . ." Cravens looked up, ". . . you'll be our utility player. We'll try you on second. Deckard will pitch."

Utility player! Scrapper's knuckles turned white as he balled his hands into tight fists. And batting eighth! It was all he could do to keep his mouth shut.

"Okay. That's all for today. Go home, get a good night's sleep and be back here by noon. That'll give us plenty of time to loosen up before the game."

Ray Hargis fell into step beside Scrapper as they left the locker room. His dark brown eyes sparkled and he couldn't keep from grinning. "Think of it, Mitch. Our first game in Triple-A ball! It's a long way from those dinky Double-A parks."

Scrapper remained silent as Ray rattled on.

"Wish the folks back home could see me now. I was batting champ on the high school team but this . . . this . . . well, this was something I only dreamed about. What do you think our chances are for making it to the big leagues?"

Scraps shrugged his shoulders. "As good as anyone's, I guess."

"Yeah. There's only one thing bothers me. The competition here is stiffer than in Double-A. There's a lot of pressure."

Scrapper wasn't worried about competition. He thrived on it. It always sparked him to do his best. But he had seen other ballplayers get so uptight that they couldn't do anything right. Maybe Hargis was one of those.

"Be cool," he said. "Just forget about it and do your job. You'll be okay."

"'Be cool,' the man says." Ray spread his arms in a helpless gesture. "I bet I don't close my eyes all night."

"You will," predicted Scrapper. And he was right. Ray fell asleep almost as soon as his head hit the pillow.

It was Scrapper who lay awake. *Utility player! Batting eighth!* rang through his head. It was almost dawn before Scrapper decided what he was going to do.


Cravens kept his players in the locker room until the stands were almost full. He always gave them a last minute pep talk but this time he stretched it out. When he saw they were getting restless, he waved them toward the tunnel and yelled, "Go get 'em!" As they ran past him, he clapped his hands and urged, "Hustle! Hustle!"

The hometown fans rose to their feet with a roar as the first White Sox player ran on to the field. By the time the last one had appeared, the applause was deafening. Cravens smiled. That was the effect he wanted. Noise had a lot to do with a team's confidence.

The Portland Twins were first at bat. Scrapper ran out to second base, tagged up for good luck, and took a stance behind the base line. It was easier to charge a ball if it came his way than to run backward to catch up with it. He leaned forward, arms swinging loosely, ready to move in either direction.

Deckard walked the first batter and Scraps moved closer to second base, ready for a throw from the catcher if the base runner tried to steal. The second batter hit a clean single past Garrison, the shortstop.

*A great way to start,* thought Scrapper—*top of the first, two men on, and no outs.* He drifted off the bag in case the two men tried for a double steal. They probably wouldn't, but if they did and the ball came his way he knew he could cut off both of them. And that, he thought, is what you call strategy. But Deckard bore down and the next man hit an infield fly to the pitcher, forcing the runners to remain on base. The next two he struck out.

Scraps sat in the dugout and watched his own team do no better. During the next two innings, only one chopper came his way. He fielded it with a quick hop for the out to first. He was getting bored and frustrated.

His turn at bat came in the bottom of the third. Cravens gave him the signal to bunt. But when a long, lazy, waist-high ball floated toward him, he drew back and slugged it into right field for a hit. Keyed up, he took a long lead and sprinted for second when the pitcher let go of the ball, sliding in and popping to his feet in one fluid motion. The crowd shouted its approval.

Each time the pitcher turned his back on him, Scraps darted partway down the base line. The crowd caught his enthusiasm. A burly man in a cutoff T-shirt stood up, punched his fist forward, and yelled, "Go! Go!" Then others began to take up the chant until the stadium rang.

Scrapper played to the fans, tagging up and trotting back each time the pitcher hurled one in. And each time he did, the Twins third baseman covered the bag, his glove raised for a throw from the catcher.

Scraps was almost a third of the way down the line when a teammate hit a liner through the hole and into short center field. He took off. The third base coach raised his arms for him to hold up there. Scraps ignored the signal.

Rounding the base, he lit out for home, diving in under the catcher's mitt and scoring the first run for the Sox. The fans cheered wildly, but when Scrapper headed back to the dugout, he found Cravens, his face red, waiting for him.

"When I tell you to bunt, Mitchell, you bunt!"

"It wasn't a bunt pitch, Coach," said Scrapper. "That ball was just waiting to be hit. I couldn't pass it up."

"You'll pass up anything I tell you to pass up!

And that includes taking an extra base. Is *that* understood?"

"Yeah, sure." Scrapper shrugged his shoulders but couldn't resist adding, "I got us on the scoreboard, though. That's more than anyone else had done."

"It was a stupid thing to do." Cravens's eyes narrowed as he continued, "You aren't playing against a bunch of high school rookies now. Most of these players are seasoned professionals. If the throw to home hadn't been on the wrong side of the plate, you'd have been out a mile. If there's one thing we don't need on this team, it's a hotdog. You got that, Mitchell?"

"Yeah. Sure." Scrapper didn't argue.

Cravens jerked his thumb toward the bench but Scrapper didn't have time to sit down. The inning over, he picked up his glove and trotted out to second.

The Twins' first batter popped up between second and third. Garrison signaled for the catch, but Scrapper darted in front of him and caught it for the out.

"What's with you?" asked Garrison angrily. "That was my ball. You almost ran into me."

"Yeah? 'Almost' don't count, man," said Scrapper with a cocky grin.

Garrison frowned but said nothing more. The second batter was at the plate. Deckard took him to the three-two count and then sent him down with a sinker. The next man grounded out to first.

Scrapper had nothing to do but watch while his team batted. He could feel Garrison glance at him from time to time but it didn't bother him.

In the top of the fourth the Twins scored one

run on a long fly ball over the right field fence.
Though there was no infield action, only two more
hard hits, which the outfielders caught on the fly.
The Sox put two men on base in the bottom of the
inning but weren't able to bring them in. The ball
game was tied one to one.

The Twins' first batter, a left-hander, tried for a
bunt and missed it for strike one. Scrapper moved
in toward second, expecting the same swing.
Again the batter missed, but Scrapper stayed near
his own base. Lefties were more apt to hit into left
field and he wanted to be ready.

On the next pitch, the batter drew back and
sent a bouncer straight for the shortstop. Scrapper
dived for it, forcing Garrison to swerve to keep
from running over him. Scraps jumped to his feet
and made the play at first.

Most of the fans cheered, but a few, aware that
Scrapper was stealing his teammate's plays,
booed his unsportsmanlike conduct.

The next man got on base with a Texas Leaguer
that dropped into midcenter field.

"How come you didn't get that one, Mitchell?"
asked Garrison out of the corner of his mouth.

Scrapper answered with a grin.

With a man on first, he stuck close to his base,
ready for a steal or a throw from any of the other
fielders. When that throw came he scooped it up,
swung his arm to the left, and tagged the base
runner's leg as he slid in.

"Safe!" cried the umpire.

"Safe? What d'ya mean *safe*?" yelled Scrapper.
"He was out a mile!"

"He was safe." The ump glowered at Scrapper.
"He slid in under your glove."

"My glove was on the ground, man! Open your eyes! How could he go *under* it?" Scrapper, his hands on his hips, faced the umpire squarely.

By now everyone's attention was riveted on the argument at second base. Cravens left the dugout and jogged toward second, but before he could get there Scrapper slammed his glove down, and the umpire jerked his thumb toward the White Sox dugout, throwing Mitchell out of the game.

Grumbling about the unfair call, Scrapper picked up his glove and stomped off the field.

"Take a shower," said Cravens, when Scrapper passed him. "A cold one."

After the game ended with a 2–1 win for the Sox, the team hustled into the locker room. Scrapper was sitting opposite a wall, bouncing a ball against it.

"Who-o-o-e-e-e!" Deckard wiped his forehead. "We just barely pulled that one off."

"Yeah," said Scrapper, catching the ball in his mitt and heading for his locker, "and I guess you know where that winning run came from."

"Cool it, Mitch," said Hargis, glancing around nervously at the other players, who had suddenly become very quiet.

"I calls 'em as I sees 'em," said Scrapper, turning his back on the room and reaching into his locker for his jacket. Then he slammed his locker door and stormed out.

Hargis sat down heavily and began to unlace his cleats. He kept his eyes down but he could hear some of the other players murmuring among themselves. Garrison was doing most of the talking. When Scrapper's name came up, Hargis knew they were planning something.

# THREE

Since there was no one to meet him at the Pawtucket, Rhode Island airport, David "DT" Green hailed a cab and went directly to Boston's AAA ballpark. There he stood in the shadows feeling awkward with his suitcase in his hand and watched the Pawtucket Red Sox practice.

Phil Sisko, the Sox manager—a tall, spare man with a perpetual frown—finally spotted him and motioned him over.

Scowling, he looked David up and down. "You're Green," he stated. "You're also late. Practice started an hour ago. Get dressed and take center field."

David started to explain that he had just arrived but Sisko interrupted.

"Vint!" shouted the manager. A blond boy about David's age trotted over.

"Get Green a uniform . . . and a locker," ordered Sisko.

Bobby Vint, Sox right fielder, nodded and said, "This way."

Sisko watched the two boys leave the playing area. He hated the beginning of the season. Breaking in new players was tough on everyone. Most of them were either too cocky or too timid. Sometimes it took weeks for them to fit in. He wondered how long it would take Green.

When they reached the locker room, Vint, a three-year veteran of the Pawtucket team, pointed out an empty locker. Then he studied David's six-foot-five frame and shook his head. "We're a little short on large sizes right now. The new ones aren't here yet. But I'll see what I can do." He disappeared into a supply room.

"Thanks," David called after him. "This is all kind of new to me. Triple-A ball, I mean." He set down his suitcase and stripped off his shirt.

"Here, try these on," Vint said, tossing Green a shirt, pants, and socks.

David nodded and pulled on the uniform pants. "A little short," he said, as he stood and tugged the socks up and the pant legs down until they met. "Reminds me of Little League."

Vint smiled. DT picked up the shirt and held it out in front of him. "No way this will fit," he said, laughing and shaking his head. "What will Coach say if he sees me come out in a T-shirt?" Before Vint could answer, Green frowned and said, "He didn't seem very happy to see me at all."

"That was his good face," explained Bobby, grinning. "Wait'll you see him when he's really mad. But you'll get used to it. Sisko's tough but he's fair. Say," he added, deciding that he liked David Green, "my roommate left a couple of weeks ago so if you want to bunk with me, you're welcome."

"Sure," said David. "Thanks."

"Okay. Let's get back out on the field. You've got a lot of guys to meet."

When Sisko saw that David was wearing only half a uniform, he scowled.

"Best I could do, Coach," explained Bobby. "There was nothing big enough."

Sisko stared long and hard at the two boys before turning away and calling the other players in.

As they clustered around him, he nodded toward David. "Green, here, will start in center field. We'll hit some balls to him, let him get warmed up, and then see what he can do at the bat."

Pawtucket's Red Sox took in David's short pants, which had crept up over his socks. "Hey, Green, what happened to your uniform?" one player called out.

"Must've shrunk from the heat," David shot back, smiling.

Everyone let go at once with a round of good-natured laughter.

Everyone except Sisko. "Back to the field," he barked. "Paige, give us some big, round floaters. Teague, knock 'em toward center field."

David ran out, adjusted his cap to keep the sun out of his eyes, and caught fly after fly—some short, some long, some against the fence where he had to leap for the ball. By the time Sisko called a halt, his pants were above his knees and his socks had fallen down around his ankles. He trotted in.

After finding a bat he felt comfortable with, he stepped to the plate while another player covered center field. Paige began with easy pitches. David pounced on the first one, sending it over the left fielder's head. When he bounced the next one off the center field fence, the outfielders backed up. Paige began to bear down but so did David, sending three balls into the bleachers before hitting a mile-high pop fly.

Then Sisko called an end to the practice and everyone filed into the locker room.

"What are you going to wear tomorrow, Green?" asked Bruce Teague, the third baseman. He was as muscular as David and almost as tall.

"Hmm . . ." David frowned, eyeing Teague's build. Then his eyes lit up and he grinned. "Could wear yours," he suggested.

"No way, man, no way!" Teague clutched his uniform to his chest.

"Don't look at *me*," two others joined in.

David's mouth turned down at the corners. "I could play in my shorts."

"That should draw a crowd," drawled first baseman, Buddy Barber. "Attendance was down all last year."

"Yeah," chimed in Paige. "Let's go with that."

David knew they were ribbing him but he didn't mind. It meant that they had accepted him.


Wearing his new uniform, which fit perfectly, David ran out for the first of two games against the Richmond Braves and glanced up at the crowd as he took his position in center field. The stands were filling up, with hundreds of Sox caps dotting the bleachers.

"It's Cap Night," explained Bobby Vint. "Brings

out a lot of families, especially those with kids. Kids make a lot of noise and that's good—gets everyone psyched."

Bobby had played against most of the Braves before and he gave David some tips as each batter came up. "Here's Catridge," he said in the top of the third. "There are two outs but he's a long-ball hitter—usually center or right. Could go over."

Catridge, the third batter of the inning, took two before connecting for a hard, high fly into deep center. David ran back, keeping an eye on both the fence and the ball. At the last second, he leaped, snagging the ball in the webbing of his glove and turning a certain two-bagger into an out to retire the side with no hits and no one left on.

Pawtucket's fans stood up and cheered as hundreds of young boys waved their caps in the air. Vint flipped David a thumbs-up. "Not bad for a beginner," he said as they ran to the dugout. "You're first up, aren't you?"

"Yeah." David pulled on his batting helmet, slipped on his gloves to give him a better grip, and picked up his bat. He took some practice swings before stepping up to the plate. He was excited but he wasn't nervous. He would wait for his pitch.

Waiting didn't bother him like it did some batters. If the first one was in there, he'd go for it. But if it wasn't, he'd take his time, blocking out everything and everyone except himself and the pitcher. Each throw was a personal challenge and he trusted his eye and his quick reactions. Being behind didn't bother him, either. He was just as cool with two strikes against him as he was with none.

Grasping the bat loosely, he watched the first pitch whiz past his knees. When the umpire called it a strike, David rolled his eyes and looked at the man but didn't argue. Some umps called them closer than others. He'd just have to allow for that.

He fouled the next one off, back into the stands, much to the delight of the fans, who screamed and scrambled for the ball, reaching out to catch it. A young boy came up with it. He brought his bat around late on the third pitch, knocking the ball into left field for a single.

*I was slow on that,* he thought as he took first.

A wild pitch gave him time to make second in a stand-up steal. Then came a strikeout followed by another single, sending David to third.

The Sox pitcher, Paige, stepped into the batter's box. He took two before getting under one and lifting a high fly into short center. David stretched out as far as he could while still keeping one foot on the base. The second the fielder had the ball, David took off, sliding safely into home plate for his first run scored.

At the top of the batting order again, Teague grounded out to the pitcher, leaving one on.

The Braves scored one run in the next two innings while the Sox were unable to break the tie. David popped out to right field his second turn at bat.

Bobby Vint led off the bottom of the fifth with a short hopper through the hole.

Green stepped into the on-deck circle as the next Sox batter, catcher Wade Williams, went to the plate. *Come on, Wade,* he thought, *just get on base.* Keeping his eye on the pitcher, David swung as each pitch came in. The bat felt good in his hands. It was balanced just right.

When Williams got to the three-and-oh count, David looked over his shoulder at the third base coach, saw him touch his left ear and adjust his cap, the signal for Williams to take one. The catcher poised, his bat raised, and let a perfect pitch go by. Then he dug in for the next one.

*A walk*, thought David, *that's as good as a hit. Doesn't count in the record books but it'll get you on base and put Vint on second. Then if I can hit a . . .*

He didn't get to finish the thought. Williams swung at the next pitch, bouncing it to the shortstop, who covered second and fired to first for the double play.

When he stepped to the plate, David was all eyes and hands, ready to destroy the right pitch. In the second or so that it took the first pitch to reach him, he read it perfectly, leaned into it, bringing his arms around and breaking his wrists as the bat connected to send the ball in a majestic arc over the center field fence.

Sox fans jumped up and cheered wildly as he trotted around the bases to meet his teammates, who had run out of the dugout at the crack of the bat. They knew *that* one was going over.

"Talk about your long ball!" exclaimed left fielder Al Whitehall.

"Long gone!"

"Rub some of those runs off on me," said Williams, high-fiving Green. "If I hadn't hit into a double play, we'd be three up instead of one."

"Tough break," said David, slapping Williams on the back as Joe Wychinski, shortstop, flyed out to the second baseman, ending the Sox's chance for any more runs in the fifth.

Determined to pull ahead, the Braves' first batter doubled into left. When the next man hit a hard line drive into right center, David raced for it, caught it inches before it hit ground, and, still running, zinged it to the third baseman, cutting off the runner from second for two outs. Paige struck out the next man to retire the side.

For the next three innings, the score remained 2–1, with batters on both teams going down in order.

"Let's beef up that lead!" yelled Sisko from the dugout.

Whitehall started off with a looper into left field for a single. Vint followed with a routine hopper to second base, forcing Whitehall to remain on first and sending Williams to the plate.

*Here we go again,* thought the catcher, uptight. *Another double play and it's all over.* He looked back at David in the on-deck circle, wishing the center fielder were up instead of him.

He relaxed only a little when Sisko rubbed his chin and ran both hands down the front of his shirt. He wanted a bunt and Williams was a good bunter.

The first two pitches were balls, too high for bunts. A light tap of the bat would send the ball up for an automatic infield out and, with Whitehall taking a dangerous lead, he could get caught between bases and run down. The Braves pitcher, sensing Williams's indecision, hurled his change-up, low and inside.

Williams brought his bat around, holding it

horizontally. The ball bounced off for a sacrifice bunt and Whitehall took second.

*It's up to me now,* thought David, taking Wade's place at the plate. The Braves pitcher looked at him for several seconds before beginning his windup. Again the ball came in low. David let it go by and the umpire called, "Strike!"

The next three pitches were too low, for a three-and-one count. The opposing pitcher wasn't going to give David anything he could get under if he could help it.

Green backed out of the box, knocked the dirt out of his cleats with his bat, stepped back to the plate and dug in. When he saw the ball coming toward him, he couldn't believe it. It was too perfect. Lifting his right foot slightly and then coming forward with all his strength, he powered a fly ball that cleared the left field fence by ten feet.

This time his teammates met him at home base with a forearm bash.

"Who-o-o-e-e-e!"

"Way to go!"

"All-l-l-l right!"

"That one cleared the parking lot!"

"Whadda ya mean 'parking lot'? *That* one went downtown!"

DT's two RBIs were followed by two more hits. But both men were left on base when Paige struck out.

"All you gotta do is hold them," said Sisko before he turned the team loose to take the field. "I want this win and I want it bad."

*Three outs to go,* thought David as he ran into center field.

The first two outs came easy, with a foul fly and a chopper to the first baseman. Then the Braves got two on with a single and a double, putting the tying run on third, the winning, on second.

Catridge stepped in and David concentrated on what Vint had told him about the Braves batter— he hits long, usually to center or right field. DT backed up, ready to go either way.

Catridge swung hard but he got under it too much and connected for a high fly to short center. David raced forward, saw he wasn't going to reach it, and dived, his arm outstretched. The ball fell into his glove to give the Sox a victory and the fans another thrill. Their shouts rang in his ears as he headed back to the dugout and into the locker room.

"Man, you pulled that one out of the fire!" yelled Teague.

"Yeah! Two runs!"

"And that catch!"

"Su-u-u-per!"

David flushed but couldn't help grinning. It was a great start.

"Hey," said Williams, lowering his voice and looking over his shoulder, "Want to go to the beach with us?"

"The beach?" asked DT. "What for?"

"To unwind," answered Teague. "Just lie back and listen to the waves come in." He spread his arms, closed his eyes and swayed slightly as he asked in a dreamy voice, "Who's for it?"

Several players raised their hands and grinned.

"I don't know," said David. "I'm pretty tired. You going, Vint?"

"Sure. It's kind of a tradition after a win. You'll like it."

David decided he'd go along. He *was* tired but he was also wound up—too wound up to go right back to his room, even though he knew that's just what he should do.

# FOUR

Roberto had been sitting on the park bench for so long that the warped wooden slats were beginning to make his back ache. A few early-morning joggers ran past him, making the circuit of the ten-acre park.

Ramirez ignored them. He was watching the newsstand across the street, waiting for it to open. Three bundles of tightly packed newspapers had been thrown off delivery trucks onto the sidewalk in front in the last half hour. It wouldn't be long now.

When an old man unlocked the door and his young helper began to drag the bundles in, Magic stood up and headed for the building.

"Good morning," said the old man as Roberto opened the door. "Beautiful day, isn't it?"

"Yes," said Roberto absently, his eyes searching the piles of papers for the local edition.

When he spotted what he wanted, he picked up

the top issue and reached in his pocket for change.

The boy stopped his work and stared at him, openmouthed. "Hey, I know you. I saw you pitch yesterday. You . . ."

Roberto didn't give him time to finish. Tossing some coins on the counter, he bolted from the store, the paper tucked under his arm. It wasn't the first time he had been recognized, although it didn't happen very often. Albuquerque was a large city and not everyone was a Dodger fan. Any other time Roberto would have been flattered and would have taken time to talk to the boy, but not today.

Rounding a corner, he stopped and turned to the sports page, half expecting to see a picture of Billy Mills lying at home plate. There was no picture, but there was a recap of the game. It stated only that José Penara had replaced Billy Mills, who was hit by a wild pitch.

Roberto had hoped that the article might say where Billy had been taken and what his condition was. When he found nothing, he tucked the paper back under his arm and started the long walk home. Three blocks from the newsstand he passed a telephone booth. Stepping inside, he began to leaf through the Yellow Pages. When he came to the heading "Hospitals," he picked up the receiver and began to dial.

Jim Graves yawned, stretched, and rolled out of bed. He wasn't surprised that Roberto was gone. Everyone knew that Capella was in his office before 7:00 A.M., going over the stats from the day before and preparing his strategy for the upcoming game.

When Jim saw that his note was no longer on the dresser, he figured Roberto had taken it with him. He hoped the coach wouldn't be too hard on him.

He decided to leave a little early himself so he'd have time to talk to his roommate before practice.

Roberto was surprised to find Jim gone. Usually they had breakfast together and rode the bus with the other players. Thinking Jim might be in the nearby restaurant, he pushed open the door and stepped inside.

Bobby Parsons and Dennis Packard, who had the room next to theirs, sat in a corner booth. Parsons waved and motioned Roberto over.

"Thought you'd be out at the park," he said.

"At the park?" Roberto looked at his watch, wondering if it had stopped. But then he realized that it couldn't have or Parsons and Packard wouldn't still be here.

"I was looking for Graves," he said. "Has he been in?"

Bobby shook his head. "Musta left early. How come you're back here?" He frowned and looked across the table at Packard before asking, "You're still on the team, aren't you?"

"On the team?" Roberto looked confused.

"Sit down, Magic, and have some breakfast," said Packard, with a warning glance at Bobby.

"Thanks, but I'm not hungry. Catch you later." Roberto left the two staring thoughtfully after him and caught the first bus that came by.

When he got to the ball park, he found Graves in the locker room. "How bad was it?" Jim asked.

"Couldn't find out a thing," said Roberto, slumping down on a bench and leaning back against the wall. "Called every hospital in town. Finally found the one where they took him but couldn't get any information. It was too early to call the patients and they wouldn't give any progress reports except to members of the family."

Jim's eyes widened. "Hospital? Whadda ya mean? Who's in the hospital?"

"Billy Mills," said Roberto. "Wasn't anything in the 'early bird' paper, either?"

Jim ran his hand over his face and groaned. "*That's* where you've been—out buying newspapers and making phone calls?"

Roberto nodded.

"Oh, man! Cap is gonna kill you. My note said to see him early and when he says early, he means *early*—like seven A.M."

"Note? What note?"

"The one I left on the dresser. You didn't find it?" Jim's voice rose an octave.

Roberto shook his head.

"Oh, man. Now he'll skin both of us. You were supposed to see him this morning. First thing!" Graves imitated Cap's well-known scowl.

"It's not your fault." Roberto jumped up and sprinted down the corridor which led to Capella's office. No wonder Parsons and Packard had looked at him so strangely.

Taking a deep breath, he tapped lightly on the closed door.

"It's not locked, Ramirez," growled Capella. "Come in and close the door behind you."

Roberto slipped inside, wondering how Capella knew it was him. Cap didn't give him a chance to ask.

"A little late, aren't you?" he drawled, pushing his chair back and drumming his fingers on the worn desk top. "Oversleep?" He fixed Roberto with an icy stare.

"No, sir." Roberto stood straight, his feet slightly apart and his hands clasped behind him. "I didn't know you wanted to see me. It was dark when I left the motel and I didn't see Jim's note."

"Dark? You've been wandering around in the dark?"

"I . . . I wanted to see if I could find out anything about Billy Mills."

"You're not an Astro, Ramirez. Let them take care of their own. All you need to worry about is the Dodgers. I'd like to make a clean sweep of this three-game series. You'll start again tonight."

"But . . . I pitched yesterday."

"I know that," said Capella, his expression stern and unyielding. "You pitched one and a half innings. You didn't hurt your arm. What happened to you yesterday happens to every pitcher sooner or later. And the only way you're going to get over it is to go right back out there and start over. Forget it ever happened. So suit up and get out on the field."

*I'll never forget*, thought Roberto. *Never*. But how could he explain that to Cap? He just nodded and turned to go. He had his hand on the door-knob when Capella spoke again.

"Ramirez," said the coach, his tone softening, "Mills is all right. I talked to his trainer this morning. He had a light concussion and they kept him in the hospital overnight for observation. He's expected to be on the roster tonight."

Roberto felt as if a great load had been lifted from his shoulders. "Thanks," he said, closing the door softly behind him.

Capella was right about one thing. Mills *was* on the roster, but he didn't play. When the starting lineups were announced, Roberto felt his stomach tighten. And when he took the mound, it was all he could do to keep his eyes from straying to the Astro dugout where Mills sat on the bench.

His first pitch was outside, his second low. Jim signaled for an inside pitch, holding his mitt a little to his left. Roberto shook off the signal, winding up for another outside ball. With a three-and-oh count, the batter glanced toward his own coach, received the signal to take one, and let the next pitch go by for a walk.

Jim trotted out to the mound. "Take it easy, Magic. Relax. You're so tense I can feel it."

Roberto nodded. But he was more than tense—he was terrified. Walking the first batter of the game was a storm warning to Roberto—a sign that worse was to come. His stomach tied in knots, he watched the second batter step to the plate and take his stance.

When the ball whizzed by him, again on the outside, the batter moved a little closer to the plate and got ready to swing.

Roberto choked. He threw one into the ground where it hit the back of the plate and ricocheted out of Jim's reach. The runner on first advanced to second.

Roberto glanced toward Capella but the coach sat with his arms folded as he stared out into center field.

Taking off his glove, Roberto rubbed his left hand across his chest and tried to calm down as he glanced over his right shoulder at the runner on second. Then he stretched out his arms, drew his hands toward his chest and started his windup. Ball three. A low moan arose from the fans. This wasn't the Magic they were used to seeing.

Jim came back out to the mound. "Just get it over the plate, Magic. He won't swing at the next one."

Roberto nodded. He knew that. Only the very best hitters were allowed to swing on the three-and-oh count.

After another glance at the base runner, Roberto fired in a fastball over the outside corner—three and one. Jim gave him another signal for an inside pitch. This time Roberto didn't shake it off but his pitch turned outside and the batter took first.

With a sinking heart, Roberto watched the Astros' third batter, a power hitter, step up.

Astro fans, hungry for runs, sent up a wild cheer. Dodger fans held their breath.

Ramirez rubbed the back of his neck and straightened up. Steeling himself and trying to push Billy Mills out of his mind, he took Jim's signal for an inside curve. But the curve wasn't there and the ball sailed right down the middle, waist high. The batter jumped on it, blasting it into the bleachers in right field. Home run.

As all three Astros trotted in to home plate, Capella left the dugout, followed closely by a relief pitcher. To Roberto he said only, "See me after the game. *Right* after."

Roberto nodded and returned to the dugout where he spent the remainder of the game watching his team lose 3–0 to the Tucson Astros.

When he filed into the locker room with the rest of the disappointed team, no one looked his way. He didn't stop at his locker. Instead, he went straight through until he came to Capella's office, where he waited for the coach.

"Go on in, Ramirez," said Capella, sounding tired. "Have a seat." He motioned toward a wooden chair in front of his desk.

Roberto sat on the edge of the seat and waited for Capella to give him his walking papers.

And when Capella said, "You won't pitch for a while," Magic was sure that was what the coach was going to do.

Roberto looked down at his hands. He couldn't blame him.

Capella went on, "You're a good pitcher, Ramirez. You've got a lot of potential but you've also got a hang-up. How many pitches did you throw tonight?"

"Ten," mumbled Roberto, looking up. He expected to see the icy stare of that morning, but instead Capella looked troubled.

"And where were they?" asked the coach.

"Where?"

"Yes, where? Except for that last one—a big, fat floater right down the middle. Where were the others?"

Roberto winced. "They were outside, Cap."

"Exactly. Now I'm going to pitch something *your* way. Not a curve, just a fact of life. If you want to make it to the big leagues, you're going to have to throw inside pitches. If you don't, you'll never be more than a five-hundred pitcher and that's not good enough for L.A. They build their team around good pitching. You've got two choices. You can overcome your hang-up and get a chance at the big time or you can stay right here until someone better comes along. That might be next year or it might be next week. It's up to you."

Roberto knew that what Capella said was true. He just didn't know if he could overcome the paralyzing fear that had gripped him on the mound.

"Just give it your best shot. That's all I ask." Capella stood, signaling that the interview was over. After Roberto left the room, the Dodger coach remained standing for several seconds, staring thoughtfully at the closed door.

With a deep sigh and a shake of his head, he flipped through his Rolodex of telephone numbers, picked up the receiver, and began to dial.

# FIVE

Ray dressed as quickly as he could and hurried back to the motel. He was worried about Scrapper. He knew that his roommate was good enough to deserve a permanent spot on the team but he wouldn't get it by stealing plays and losing his temper. He only hoped he could make Scrapper see that.

When he found their room empty, he covered a three-block area, looking in all the fast-food places he could find until he spotted Scraps at a table back in the corner of a small all-night diner. Weaving his way to the back, he pulled out the chair opposite Scraps and sat down.

Scrapper looked up but didn't say anything.

"You all right?" asked Ray.

"Sure. Why not? I get thrown out of games every day." Underneath Scrapper's cocky grin and brash statement was a trace of bitterness.

"That *was* a bad call," said Ray. "I thought the runner was out, too."

"Let's just forget it, okay? I lost my temper, that's all. We redheads have a low boiling point. Everyone will forget it tomorrow."

Ray wished that were true but he had a sinking feeling that Scrapper's troubles were only beginning. His temper was only *part* of the problem. He was being overaggressive and hogging the show.

Ray was just as anxious as Scrapper was to get to the majors and he wanted to say so but Scraps had made it clear that he didn't want to talk about it. He sighed and picked up a plastic-covered menu. Maybe it was just a case of the new kid on the block trying too hard to be one of the gang.

"How did you do after I left?" asked Scraps, pushing away a half-eaten cheeseburger.

"Lousy," admitted Ray. "Okay in the field but I struck out twice."

"Nothing to be ashamed of," said Scrapper. "That Twins pitcher was pretty good."

"*You* got two hits," pointed out Ray.

"That's 'cause I'm terrific," boasted Scraps with a lopsided grin. "Watch me tomorrow—three for four, at least."

The next day, Ray and Glen waited with the other players to hear the starting lineup. Ray's locker was next to Scrapper's so he sat down on the bench while his roommate laced his cleats. The other players brushed past them without talking, anxious to get out on the field.

"Go ahead, Hargis," said Scraps. "There's no use you getting the cold shoulder, too."

Ray started to protest when Cravens entered, clipboard in hand. "We're going with the same starters as last night," said the coach, "with one exception. I'm putting Stevens in at second. Mitchell sits this one out."

"Sit it out?" asked Scrapper, flushing with anger. "I'm not playing?"

"That's what I said." Cravens fixed him with a cold stare before waving the others out.

Scrapper gritted his teeth, followed his teammates out, and went directly to the dugout where he sat on the far end of the bench, his arms crossed. He didn't speak to the other players nor look their way. There was a lot of chatter while the Sox batted but Scrapper didn't join in.

When Stevens, the second baseman, missed a routine play, allowing a man to score, Scraps felt his temper soar. *I would've had that*, he thought angrily.

The Sox put up a good fight but lost by two runs.

In the locker room, Cravens said nothing about Stevens's error but he did single out Ray, who had gone oh for three. "You need batting practice, Hargis. I want you in the cage first thing tomorrow morning."

Ray nodded and turned to Scrapper. "Sometimes I don't even see the ball," he whispered. "And when I do, it's past me before I know it."

"There's more to a game than batting," said Scraps. "You'll get the hang of it." He raised his voice, adding, "If I'd been playing, we would have won."

"What is that supposed to mean?" Stevens responded angrily.

Scrapper shrugged but didn't back off. "Just what I said. With my batting, fielding, and stealing, we would have won."

Garrison, his eyes flashing, took a step toward Scrapper. "With your stealing bases or stealing plays?" he asked.

Two teammates flanked him, and all three glared at Mitchell.

"Cool it, Mitch," warned Ray, looking nervously from Glen to the three other players and back again.

Scrapper shrugged, stuffed his clothes into his locker, slammed the door shut, and stalked out of the room.

"Whatcha doin' up so early?" Glen asked, turning on the bedside light to see what time it was.

"Batting practice." Ray ran a comb through his hair.

"Hey, it's still dark out."

"Sun'll be up the time I get out to the park."

Scrapper groaned, pushed the covers back, and swung his legs over the side of the bed. "Wait a minute and I'll go with you. You won't do any good hitting fungoes by yourself. You need someone to pitch to you."

Ray wouldn't have asked for Scrapper's help but he was grateful. He knew his roommate was right.

When they got to the ball park, the sun was low on the horizon, casting eerie shadows across the infield.

"Kind of spooky, isn't it?" said Ray, lowering his voice to keep echoes from bouncing back at him.

"Spooky?" Scrapper grinned. "Not to me. I love it—with or without a crowd." Then in a half whisper, more to himself than to Ray, he added, "I don't know what I'd do if I couldn't play baseball."

"Mitch . . ." began Ray, thinking about the past two days.

"Grab a bat!" interrupted Glen. "We're wastin' time."

Scrapper went out to the mound, threw a few pitches to Ray to loosen up, and then told him to get set. "I can throw pretty hard," he said, "but I'm no pitcher so get ready to duck if you see one comin' right at you."

Ray laughed. "Don't worry, I will," he said.

Mitchell had never really watched Ray bat, and after his roommate missed several easy pitches, he began to see what was wrong.

Leaving the mound, he walked to home plate and said, "Let me see that bat."

"I think it has a hole in it," said Ray wearily, handing the bat over.

The minute Scrapper took it, he knew what one of Ray's problems was. "This is too heavy for you. No wonder you're not gettin' around on the ball. Get a lighter one."

As Ray ran to the dugout and picked out a lighter bat, Scrapper tried to remember everything his father had taught him about batting.

"That's better," he said when Ray handed him the lighter bat. "Now when you get to the plate, hold the bat in your fingers, not the palms of your hands. Like this." He held the bat out for Ray to see what he meant. "Then stand with your feet shoulder-width apart, toes toward the plate, head up." Again he illustrated. "You're standing almost sideways, which means that if you do hit the ball, you won't have your body behind it."

Ray nodded and took the bat. "It feels different," he said, standing in as Scrapper had shown him and taking a few cuts in the air, "but better."

"It'll work, too." Scrapper loaded his pockets with balls. "Just hold the bat upright and swing down slightly."

He started back to the mound but stopped halfway there and offered another bit of advice. "Watch the ball. Look at my cap until just before the pitch. Then shift your focus to my hand."

Scrapper started with slow pitches to let Ray get the feel of the lighter bat and different stance. Then he bore down. Many of his pitches were balls but when one did get in there, Ray sent it flying.

"Much better," said Scrapper after Ray had hit five in a row. "Time to stop," he added as White Sox players began to drift out onto the field.

Ray left the plate and went to the cage. He was a little nervous with Cravens standing right behind him until he saw Scrapper give him an "okay" sign. Then he settled down.

Cravens watched Ray closely as he batted. "Nice going," the coach said after Ray connected for four hits. "You look like a different batter."

"Thanks," said Ray. "I got some good tips from Mit—"

"Hargis!" cried Scrapper, running up and shaking his head. "How 'bout hitting some grounders my way? I could use the fielding practice."

Why didn't you want me to tell him?" asked Ray as he and Scrapper walked down the right base line. "It might have helped you, too."

Mitchell shook his head again. "Teammates are supposed to help each other." He wanted back on the team, wanted it more than anything else, but not that way. He was going to make it for what he could do on the field and at the plate, not for what he could do for someone else.

"Let's go early," said Ray that afternoon. "I want to practice those batting tips you gave me."

Scrapper, who was lying on his bed, hands under his head, smiled at his roommate.

Ray was watching himself in the mirror, making sure that he had the right stance and then bringing an imaginary bat around.

"You go ahead," said Scraps. "I'll catch ya later."

Ray met Scrapper's eyes in the mirror. "Don't be late, okay? Cravens gets real mad about that and you're already on his list."

"Yeah, I know. I'll be there in time, Kid. Don't worry."

The last thing he wanted to do was get to the park early. The less time he had to spend with his teammates, the better. He knew that if anyone mouthed off to him in the locker room, he'd get in trouble, so he planned on getting there at the last minute.

When he did arrive, he heard the usual chatter as he came through the door, but the minute he entered the room it died down. Most of the players pushed past him silently and headed for the field. Those who were still getting dressed, stuffed their shirttails into their pants, grabbed their caps, and hurried after their teammates.

Scrapper had the room to himself. "Who cares?" he mumbled as he began to change.

"Where is everyone?" asked Cravens, entering from the back and looking around the deserted room.

"They went on out," said Scrapper.

"Well, hurry up. You're starting tonight."

"I am?" Scrapper sat up, surprised. "Where?"

"Second. That *is* your position, isn't it?"

"Yeah, yeah, it is." Scraps threw his street clothes into his locker, slammed the door, and grabbed his cap. As he followed Cravens out, he promised himself that he'd play it straight, do the best he could, and not spout off.

The Sox started in the field. Scrapper thought something was up when he saw the first and third basemen playing wide. Then when Garrison, at short, drifted over toward second, he knew it. They were going to cut him off.

*All right,* he thought angrily, *if that's the way you want it, I'll play deep.* Pretending not to notice what was happening, he backed up into shallow center field. Only one ball came near him in the first inning—a high pop fly. Ray ran in, called for it, and caught it while Scrapper stood still and watched.

Then Garrison scooped up a ground ball in the second inning and threw the batter out at first. Another bouncer, which Scrapper would have fielded if he'd been in his usual spot, was snagged by the first baseman while the pitcher ran over to cover first.

The Sox scored two runs in the bottom of the third, one on a line drive by Hargis, who came back to the dugout grinning. "It worked!" he said, flopping down next to Scrapper. "I did it like you said and it worked!"

Scrapper nodded, only half listening. His mind was on other things.

The Twins started the fourth with a runner on first. Then came a fielder's choice. Garrison darted to his right, made a clean play, and looked toward second. Scrapper, playing deep, dashed in. It would be close but he knew he could make it.

Garrison didn't give him the chance. He threw to first for the out.

*Always cut off the lead runner!* thought Scrapper, his temper flaring. *What does Garrison think he's doing?* But he knew the answer to that. The shortstop wanted to make him look bad. They all did. If Scraps had been covering second, the throw would have gone to him with a good chance for a double play. But because he was out too far, the Twins had a man in scoring position.

Then the Sox pitcher ended the scoring threat with two strikeouts.

By the time Scraps came to bat, he was so uptight that he swung at the first pitch, so low that it hit the dirt behind home plate. He reached for the next one and stumbled forward when he didn't connect. He was trembling so badly by the third pitch that he let it go by for strike three.

In the dugout he sat with his head down for the rest of the inning. He wasn't angry. He just felt empty and alone.

The White Sox squeaked out a victory in the bottom of the ninth with another base hit by Ray. Scrapper was oh for three at the plate, and had gone zero for zero in the field. He hadn't even handled the ball.

While his teammates buzzed among themselves, Scrapper showered and dressed. He caught several sly glances, as if the others were waiting for him to say that they won because he was back in the game.

That night he lay awake long after Ray had fallen asleep, thinking about the team and his future in baseball. If he had one, that is. At 1:00 A.M. he got up, dressed, and stole out of the room, heading for an all-night diner with a phone.

There was only one person who might be able to help him straighten out the mess he'd gotten himself into. That is, if Glen decided to ask him for advice.

# SIX

Wade Williams turned the van into McDonald's, braked at the order post, and asked for sixteen Big Macs with fries and Cokes. A scratchy, metallic voice repeated the order.

"Pass your dough up," Wade yelled as he pulled around the building to the pickup window.

David and Bobby dug in their pockets, pulled out some crumpled bills and sent them forward.

"How much farther is it?" asked David.

"Couple o' blocks. Soon's we turn the corner, you'll see the ocean. Shouldn't be too crowded this time o' day. Sun's almost down."

In fact, the beach was almost deserted. Family groups had long since gone home and only a few young couples dotted the shoreline.

Carrying their sacks and soft drinks, the boys found a spot away from the teenagers, and sitting cross-legged in a semicircle, began to eat.

Vint wolfed down his two sandwiches and fries

in record time, rubbed his stomach, and sighed. "Better," he said, "much better."

"One thing I wanta know, Green," asked Al Whitehall, gathering up empty cartons and cups. "How do you get that extra zing that sends the ball over the fence?"

"Hey!" scolded Teague. "No baseball, remember? That's one of our rules," he explained for David's benefit. "We leave our bats and gloves back at the dugout."

"Just this one time," insisted Whitehall. "Then we'll drop it."

"It's all in the wrists," said David, laughing. Drawing his arms back as if he were holding a bat, he brought both hands around and broke his wrists at an imaginary pitch.

"You're not supposed to do that," said Teague, interested in spite of himself. "Coach says it makes you lose power."

"You do if you break your wrists too soon," said David. "The trick is to wait until a split second before you connect. It's all in the timing."

"My reflexes aren't that fast," said Williams.

"Neither are mine," admitted Teague, disappointed. "So let's change the subject."

For the next hour they talked about everything except baseball. Teague and Williams stretched out on the sand, adding an occassional comment as some leaned back on one elbow and others sat with arms wrapped around their knees. Then they, too, lay down until only David was left.

Even when he realized his teammates had all fallen asleep, he continued to sit up, staring out toward the sea, listening to the waves and thinking. He knew he should try to get some rest but he couldn't unwind. He thought about the last two days, relieved that he had gotten off to such a good start. He wished he could have shared those days with Magic and Scrapper.

*They'd like this*, he thought, looking up at the moon and then along the shore. There were beaches back home along Lake Michigan, too, but he had never seen them deserted—not in the summer.

He was still thinking about Magic and Scrapper, about their years together at Rosemont and how lucky they all were, when the sun peeked over the horizon. Suddenly he looked at his watch and jumped to his feet. Rubbing the kinks out of his back, he reached down and shook Bobby Vint's shoulder.

"Vint?" he asked. "It's late. We gotta be getting back."

Bobby sat up, blinking. "Uh-oh," he said, moaning. "If Sisko finds out we didn't even turn in last night, we've had it. Hey, you bozos! Wake up! Move!"

Bobby herded everyone back to the van. "You awake enough to drive, Williams?" he asked.

"Sure," answered Wade. "I always rest good on the beach."

*I wish I had*, thought David. He tried to sleep on the trip back but the swaying van and the constant flow of conversation kept jolting him awake. By the time they arrived at their motel, he was exhausted.

"What you need is a cold shower," said Vint, studying his roommate's bleary eyes.

"After you." David flopped down on his bed. He was asleep before Bobby turned on the water.

"Green! DT!" Bobby shook David awake. "Get up. We've got an hour to get to the ballpark. Practice session before the game, remember? I'm going to grab some food. Meet me in the coffee shop."

David raised up, shook his head, and dropped back down. "I'm not hungry," he mumbled. "You go on out. I'll catch ya later."

Bobby frowned and wondered if he should drag David out of bed. He decided against it but warned, "Don't go back to sleep." Then he left the room.

David glanced at the clock and thought, *A half hour. Just a few more z's. I can eat after the game.* He closed his eyes and when the phone rang an hour later, he didn't even hear it. He never did know what woke him but when he next looked at the clock, he couldn't believe that is half hour had stretched into two and a half hours.

Bounding out of bed, he stripped and took a cold shower, shivering under the icy spray until he felt wide awake. Then he called a cab. He couldn't afford one but he was running too late to worry about that.

"Side entrance," he told the driver as they pulled into a rapidly filling parking lot.

Jumping out of the taxi, he raced for the locker room, pulling off his T-shirt as he ran.

"Finally decided to put in an appearance, did you?" Sisko glowered at him from the tunnel entrance.

"Uh . . . I—" began David, his heart racing.

"No excuses, Green! When I call practice, I expect you to be here." The coach's voice was low and controlled but his eyes cut right through David like a knife.

"It won't happen again." David held his breath and wondered if Sisko would bench him. He had every right to.

"Well, what are you waiting for?" Sisko barked. "Get out there!"

"Yes, sir." David grabbed his glove and ran.

Bobby Vint met him as he came onto the field. "What kept you?" he asked. "I called a long time ago. After the eighth ring, I hung up. Thought you were on your way."

"I was out like a light," moaned David. "Didn't even hear the phone."

"You don't look awake to me," said Vint. "How do you feel?"

"Not so hot," admitted David.

"He gonna let you play?"

"Yeah. But I don't know why."

"Might have something to do with the write-up you got in the paper. The stadium is filling pretty fast and a lot of those people came out just to watch *you*."

"What do you mean?" asked David as he and Bobby ran out onto the field.

"The sports page, man! You're all over it! They're calling you the 'wonder boy'. Listen to that crowd."

David hadn't even noticed the cheering. He was too tired. But when he reached center field and turned around, he saw that Bobby was right. Hundreds of fans were standing, pointing toward him and yelling, "DT! DT!"

"Hope you can handle pressure," yelled Bobby as he trotted to right field.

David felt his stomach muscles tighten. He'd been under pressure before and it had never bothered him. But he had never tried to play on two and a half hours' sleep, either.

As the first Braves batter stepped to the plate, David hoped that the play would be anywhere except center field. Twisting to his left and then his right, he blinked and tried to stir up some energy, but it didn't help much.

*I probably won't get to bat until the second inning,* he thought. *I've got to get with it before then.*

He lucked out the first inning. There was one fly ball to center field, but it came right to him. It was in the top of the second that Catridge came up, and David ran into trouble.

Catridge hit a hard line drive to right center. Green started to move, saw Vint racing toward him, and pulled up short. The ball bounced a few feet in front of him for a hit.

*Damn, I should have had that!* thought David.

The only thing that got them out of the inning without the Braves scoring was good defense from the other players.

"That was your ball, Green," said Sisko sourly in the dugout. "Wake up."

David nodded, picked up a wet towel and scrubbed his face before grabbing his bat and running to the on-deck circle.

Williams bunted down the third base line for a clean hit and David stepped forward. The crowd began to chant, "DT! DT!"

The first pitch was so wide that the catcher had

to jump to the side to reach it. But the next one, a fastball, right down the middle, chest high—a home run pitch—sailed by him for a strike. He stepped out of the batter's box and took four hard swings, trying to loosen his stiff arms. He knew he should have pegged that one. Then he stepped back in.

Another wide pitch went by—two and one. David tensed. The next one would be in there. It was. But he hesitated too long and swung too late.

His heart began to pound. He clenched the bat, his knuckles turning white. *Watch for the change-up,* he told himself.

Squinting at the pitcher, he dug in. As the ball, a sidearm curve, headed toward him, he swung, leaning away for a grounder to the third baseman.

Then Wychinski and Valdez got on base with two singles but Paige and Teague struck out, ending the inning with three on.

"Lots of time yet," said Vint as he and David took the field.

"Yeah." Green was determined not to get caught off guard again and when a hit came his way, he went for it, racing to his left and reaching out as the ball came down. It dropped short of his glove and before he could stop his forward motion, his foot hit the ball, kicking it out of his reach. By the time he could chase it down, the runner had slid safely into second and David was charged with an error.

"Hang loose, man," called Vint softly. "You're tied up in knots."

A disappointed grumble arose from the fans.

DT tried to relax but he couldn't. He had never bobbled a ball like that before—not even in Little

League. As the runner crossed home plate on another double, he felt that it was his fault. When the inning ended, he ran into the dugout and glanced at Sisko. The coach glared at him, made some notes on his clipboard, and looked away.

David sank down on the bench, relieved that Sisko hadn't pulled him. He knew he would hear about his defense later, but at least he would get to bat again, get a chance to make up for his mistakes.

The Sox's first batter, Buddy Barber, chopped one past the shortstop to start off the bottom of the third with a single. Whitehall followed with a sacrifice fly that sent Barber to second. Vint stepped to the plate and took two before a wild pitch caught him in the left shoulder and sent him to first.

"Go get 'em, Williams," shouted David, as the catcher left the on-deck circle and headed for the plate. "It's our chance to pull ahead."

Williams, overanxious, swung at the first pitch and caught a piece of it for a foul tip into the catcher's mitt.

"Your turn," he said, trotting back past David to the dugout.

*Two on and two out*, thought David. wiping his forehead and adjusting his batting helmet. He felt a little better but still not up to par. Taking three hard cuts to loosen up, he stepped into the batter's box and faced the pitcher, his bat poised, his knees slightly bent, his eyes on the pitcher's cap.

The windup began. David leaned to his left, ready to charge forward at the ball. The first pitch looked good. He started to go for it, checking his swing at the last minute as the ball dropped before it crossed the plate.

*A little higher,* he thought, *so I can get under it, lift it up and out.* He got the pitch he wanted on the next throw and he did get under it—too much, sending it in a sky-high arc that gave the right fielder plenty of time to drift over for the out.

"Tough break," said Teague sympathetically when David returned to the dugout for his glove.

"Yeah," David mumbled before trotting out to center field. In the next two innings, he had only one play, a line drive that he didn't even have to jump for. It had his name on it.

His third time at bat he fouled off two and got caught on a change-up for a call strike three. By the end of the eighth, the Braves were still leading 1–0.

Whitehall led off with a double against the center-field fence and the Sox's hopes soared. Vint popped up but Williams plugged one through the hole, sending Whitehall to third. The Sox catcher took a long lead on first.

After a wide outside ball to Green, the Braves pitcher fired to first. Williams scrambled back safely. The count was two and oh when Williams broke for second, diving head first as the Braves catcher threw wide, pulling his second baseman off the bag.

*All right!* thought David, swinging the bat and flexing his wrists. Stepping into the next pitch, he drove the ball straight back to the pitcher, who sidestepped and snapped it up, ending the game with a 1–0 loss for the Sox.

\*   \*   \*

"Can't win 'em all," said Vint after everyone dragged back to the locker room.

"Should have had that one, though," grumbled Barber. "Had enough chances."

"Bad luck," said Teague, with a sidelong glance at David.

*Not bad luck,* thought DT, slumping onto the bench and staring at the floor. *Bad playing. Especially me—oh for four and two errors.*

He felt so miserable that he didn't realize how quiet the room was until Sisko's cold voice bounced off the walls. "Four o'clock tomorrow!" he bellowed. "Be here!" Then he turned and stomped toward his office.

A few groans punctuated the silence. "Tomorrow's a rest day," complained Wychinski.

"Not around here," said Valdez. "We're just lucky he didn't call a wake-up practice."

"Hey," said Vint, perking up. "That's right. We don't have to get up early so how about the beach tonight? Who's for it?"

"Count me in."

"Me, too."

"You got it."

Bobby looked at David. "DT?"

David shook his head. "Better not."

"We won't stay all night this time," said Bobby, grinning. "Come on. Lighten up, man."

David wished he *could* be as laid back as Vint.

"How 'bout it?" urged his roommate.

David hesitated. What harm could it do?

# SEVEN

When Roberto got back to the locker area after his talk with Cap, he found the room deserted. It was just as well. He didn't feel like talking to anyone.

He was about to leave the stadium when Jim, who had been waiting near a concession stand, called out to him. "Magic! Wait up!"

Roberto halted, wishing his roommate had gone on without him.

"Cap can be pretty tough sometimes," said Jim as he fell into step beside the pitcher. "I should know. Cap's chewed me out more than once."

Roberto nodded and followed him out of the deserted ballpark to the corner where they caught a bus back to the motel.

"How 'bout some food?" asked Jim.

Roberto glanced toward the adjacent restaurant, saw several of his teammates inside and said, "You go on. I'm not hungry."

He pretended to be asleep when his roommate

came in but it was almost dawn before he finally dozed off.

Roberto sat on the bench during the last game in the Dodgers–Astros series. He didn't begin to relax and pay attention to the game until he saw Billy Mills step up to bat. Rubbing his hands with dirt, then taking a few practice swings, Mills crowded the plate and waited for his pitch. The other Dodger pitcher, Parsons, struck him out.

"Nice going, Parsons!" Ramirez yelled, happier that Mills was playing again than for the strikeout. He knew he'd be able to concentrate on his pitching again.

The game turned out to be close, with the Dodgers pulling out a 5–4 win in the ninth.

They had a two-day rest period before the next game—against the Las Vegas Padres. Most of the first day they spent practicing. Roberto warmed up gradually until he was firing the ball so hard that at one point his catcher rocked back on his heels.

With Capella's words, "You'll never make it to the big time if you don't throw inside pitches," ringing in his ears, he covered the entire area of the strike zone, throwing outside, inside, shoulder-high and knee-high, with curve balls, fastballs, sinkers, and change-ups.

"Nice, Ramirez," said Cap from behind him. "You're starting the next game. That's the kind of pitching I want to see. Wrap it up now. No use in overworking."

"Okay, Coach." Roberto tucked his glove under his arm and headed for the locker room, smiling. He knew that Cap didn't hand out compliments very often.

He should have hung around until practice was over for everyone but he didn't. Instead, he splurged, rented a car, and drove up into the mountains.

There he sat for a long time looking out over the city of Albuquerque, his thoughts ranging from his early days of baseball in the Dominican Republic to Rosemont High to his present position with the Dodgers. When he heard children laughing as their parents warned them to stay away from the edge, he thought of his own family. He missed them.

"Try to get some rest," said Capella after his team had climbed on the bus and settled down. "You're going to need it. They're predicting one hundred ten by this afternoon. The heat will sap you."

Several of the Dodgers groaned.

Roberto, thinking of his island home, looked at his seatmate, Jim Graves. "I'm used to heat," he said.

"Not this kind," warned Jim. "Just wait. The Padres have more than the homefield advantage. They're adjusted to that scorching heat. We're not."

Roberto saw what Jim meant when he climbed off the air-conditioned bus at the Padres' stadium. The sudden change of temperature was like stepping into a blast furnace, the sun so bright that he could hardly keep his eyes open. And when he felt the heat penetrating the soles of his shoes, he hopped from one foot to the other.

"When does it cool off?" he asked.

Jim laughed. "It'll be better when the sun goes down. Not good, but better."

Roberto was thinking about their conversation as he dressed for the game. The sun was low on the horizon but heat still radiated from asphalt and concrete.

"Ramirez!" Capella's voice echoed through the tunnel leading to the playing field.

Roberto hurried out of the locker room, expecting some last minute advice.

"Over here," said Capella, who had moved to the far end of the bullpen.

Beside him stood a tall man, whose black curly hair, although shorter, was much like Magic's.

"Dad?" Roberto blinked against the lowering sun.

Mr. Ramirez laughed and hugged Roberto to him. Then stepping back and holding him at arm's length, said, "I thought it was about time I watched my son play Triple-A ball."

"I'll leave you two alone," said Capella, heading toward the tunnel.

Roberto watched him go, frowned, and faced his father. "He called you, didn't he?"

Mr. Ramirez looked down at the ground before admitting, "Yes. He told me you'd been having some problems. But he didn't ask me to come out here," he added hastily. "That was my own idea."

"It's terrific!" Roberto said. But while he was happy to see him, he knew that having his dad there was only going to add more pressure.

* * *

"Go get 'em, Magic!" Graves clapped Roberto on the back and began to strap on his catcher's gear.

The knot in Roberto's stomach grew as he got behind the first batter for a two-and-oh count. He walked around behind the mound, wiped his hands on his pants, toed the rubber and was about to begin his windup when the batter stepped out of the box.

Trying to keep his eyes off his father, Roberto waited for the batter to get set, then delivered one in there for a chopper to the right side. Dennis Packard short-hopped and threw the runner out.

The Padres' second batter swung at a breaking ball chest-high and popped out to shallow center field. Roberto walked around the mound again and wiped the sweat from his forehead with his shirtsleeve.

Sensing the pitcher's nervousness, the Padres' third batter stepped out of the box just as Roberto began to make his move. Checking his windup before it could be called a balk, he waited, wondering if the batter was deliberately trying to spook him. When the man stepped out again, Roberto was sure of it.

Hie mouth set in a grim line, he sent a fastball right down the middle. The batter brought his wood around and held it waist high, connecting for a drag bunt down the first base line. Roberto raced for first, covering it as his own first baseman chased down the ball and threw the runner out to retire the side.

"Three up and three down," said Jim, flopping down beside Roberto in the dugout. He didn't bother to remove his shin guards. He was batting eighth.

The Dodgers scored one run in the first to give them the lead and Roberto went back to the mound. His second inning was a replay of the first. His pitching wasn't bad but it wasn't spectacular. His mouth was dry. Heat waves shimmered from the roof over the stands. He wondered if he could last nine innings.

In the dugout, he splashed his face with cold water and poured a small amount down the back of his neck. Then he leaned back and closed his eyes. The team was giving him all the help it could but what he needed was strikeouts.

*I won't get them that way*, thought Roberto as the first man he faced in the top of the third hit a hard line drive into right field for a single.

Keeping an eye on the runner at first, Roberto sent in a slider, forcing the batter to jump out of the way. The baserunner took off and Roberto stepped to the side as Jim fired to second base. It was a close play but the ump's crossed arms signaled "safe."

With a man in scoring position, Roberto knew it was now or never. His next two pitches were fastballs, fouled into the bleachers behind home plate. Winding up, he delivered a breaking ball over the outside corner. The batter connected, sending the ball down the middle. It passed Roberto like a shot.

With a man now on first and third, the Las Vegas fans erupted in a wild cheer. Roberto stole a look toward Capella but the coach's face was expressionless.

One glance over his shoulder and Roberto

turned quickly to send a sidearm pitch streaking by the batter and into the dirt at Jim's feet for ball one. His next pitch was wild. Jim walked out to the mound.

"Take your time, Magic. Don't rush it."

But Roberto knew he couldn't take much more time. He had to prove himself. Capella was a patient man but his own job depended upon winning ball games. And Roberto hadn't given him much help lately.

Taking a deep breath and exhaling slowly, Roberto wound up, sending another breaking ball in low for the three-and-oh count.

Thousands of fans began to chant, "Walk! Walk!"

Magic glanced over once again toward Capella, who gave him the nod to continue. Magic squared his shoulders. It was time to take over.

And he did.

Three split-fingered fastballs, two on the inside and one that nibbled the outside corner, sent the batter back to the Padres' dugout wondering what had happened.

The next two batters were just as confused as Ramirez took *them* down, leaving two men on and ending the scoring threat.

As he walked off the field, he saw his father grin and make a circle with his thumb and forefinger. Capella, too, was smiling. He had his pitcher back.

The game was far from over, though, and the heat began to tell on all of the Dodger players. They scored no more runs but with Roberto pitching his first shutout in his last four starts, they squeaked through with a 1–0 victory.

"Glad you're back, Ramirez," said Capella as

Roberto trotted past him on his way to the locker room.

"N-i-i-ice pitchin'!" cried Graves.

Others echoed the compliment as Roberto showered, dressed, and hurried outside to meet his father.

"For a while there I thought I shouldn't have come," said the older man. "I could tell it bothered you. But after those first three innings, you didn't even know I was there, did you?"

Roberto hadn't thought about it but he knew that what his father said was true. All that mattered to him on the mound was pitting his own skills against the other team—facing them and winning.

He wondered it he'd be able to hold on to that concentration when he faced Scrapper in two weeks.

# EIGHT

"I didn't wake you, did I?" asked Scrapper when his father answered the phone.

"What's wrong?" asked Joe Mitchell, ignoring his son's question. It was 2:30 in Chicago and he knew that Scraps wouldn't have called unless something *was* wrong. "You didn't get hurt, did you?" he asked anxiously.

"No. No. It's something else." Then Scrapper launched into an account of everything that had happened since he had arrived at Vancouver, including his hot-dogging.

"I know I shouldn't have, Dad, but . . . I . . ."

"You wanted to show everyone how good you were."

"Yeah. And now I don't know what to do." Scraps took a deep breath and asked, "What would *you* do?"

"The only thing you can do is be fair and play the best way you know how. It may take some time but once the others see that you're a team player and aren't trying to steal the show, they'll work with you, not against you. There's enough glory to go around, Glen, more than enough."

"I guess I was in too much of a hurry."

"And you weren't very happy about going there in the first place, were you?"

"No," admitted Scrapper, swallowing his pride. "I thought I was good enough to go right up from spring training."

"You are good enough," insisted Joe. "Don't worry. You'll get the call. You're a better player than I was."

Scrapper ran his free hand through his hair and closed his eyes. "I had a good teacher," he said softly. A year ago he couldn't have said that, even though he had always known it was true. He winced, remembering the resentment he used to feel toward his father.

"You still there?" asked Joe.

"Yeah. I was just thinking."

"I thought you'd gone to sleep."

"No, but I *am* keeping you up. Next time I won't call so late."

"Any time, Scraps, any time."

Scrapper smiled. His father hadn't called him "Scraps" for a long time. Feeling better, he promised to let his father know how he was getting along, hung up, and returned to his room, where he fell asleep.

With only one day off before they hit the road for a game against the Calgary Mariners, Cravens called a hard practice.

"You'll have time to rest on the vans plus a few hours in the motel before we take the field," he said. "The Mariners have a hotshot pitcher and they'll probably start him. I want you to be ready."

Scrapper flinched at the word "hotshot." It sounded too much like "hot dog." He glanced around at his teammates but no one was looking his way. They were all intent on Cravens's instructions.

During practice, Scrapper started at third, then was switched to short. He glanced uneasily at Garrison but the regular shortstop didn't complain.

Still, he didn't feel comfortable until he took over second. He fielded several balls there, sticking closely to his own territory and keeping his mouth shut. No one crowded him and he began to relax.

In the cage, he forgot everyone except the pitcher—hitting ground balls, line drives, and flies. Very few balls got past him.

"That's it!" called Cravens, walking out to the middle of the infield. As the players clustered around him, he read off their weaknesses and strengths. Scrapper held his breath.

"Hargis is doing much better at the bat. I'm moving him up to third in the lineup."

Ray shot a sidelong glance at Scrapper and started to open his mouth but Scraps shook his head again.

"Mitchell! Where's Mitchell?" asked Cravens.

"Back here, Coach." Scrapper waved his arm until Cravens spotted him behind the taller players.

"You'll stay on second. That seems to be your

best position. Also . . . I'm moving you up to sixth in the batting order."

"After yesterday?" asked Scrapper, astonished. "I was oh for three."

"I'm not saying this will be permanent, but you batted well enough today to move you up. That's all for now." The coach walked off the mound and the players followed him into the locker room.

"You *ought* to move up," said Ray on the way in.

"Yeah," said Deckard. "You hit almost everything I threw at you."

"Thanks, guys," said Scrapper, wishing that the older players felt the same way.

"How about a movie tonight, Mitch?" asked Ray as he pulled on his socks. Before Scrapper could answer he raised his voice and asked, "Anyone want to go with us?"

Catcher Kurt Brown looked up and shrugged, "Why not? How about you, Fuller?"

"Sure."

"I can't," said third baseman, Tony Perez. "If I don't get a letter in the mail tonight, Mom's gonna stop sending those chocolate chip cookies." He clutched his chest and rolled his eyes.

In the end, everyone except Perez went. After the show, they stopped at the diner for a burger before calling it a night.

"See ya!" rang across the courtyard as they went to their rooms. A traveler in room 3 opened his door and looked out to see what was going on.

"Guess we were kinda loud," admitted Ray, closing the door softly after himself and Scrapper.

"Yeah," agreed Scrapper, grinning. He knew his battle wasn't over but he was beginning to make some headway. The others had been friendly toward him for the first time since he'd shown off. But the real test would come in the next game.

The trip to Calgary wasn't as long as some of their other trips, but it was tiring. The seats in the van were hard and the road was rough. Scrapper tried to sleep, but every time he dozed off he was jolted awake by the bouncing of the van. When they finally checked in at their motel, he was too wound up to relax before the game.

He wasn't the only one who was excited. He could almost feel the tension in the locker room that night. There was so little talk that Cravens didn't even have to ask them to quiet down when he came in.

"You've got your posts," he said, looking from one player to another. "Calgary has a good team, maybe the best they've fielded in a long time." He paused to give his next words more emphasis. "Let's get out there and show them what a little teamwork can do!"

Scrapper was anxious to show that he *could* be a team player if they'd give him the chance. Their attitude *was* friendlier than it had been, but that was off the field. What would it be like when they took their positions?

He found out in the bottom of the first. The Sox went down one-two-three in the top half of the inning. Cravens was right; Calgary did have a hotshot pitcher. No one had come close to hitting him.

Tagging up at second, Scrapper glanced warily at the other infielders. Fuller stayed on first, Perez hugged third, and Garrison hung midway between second and third. Scraps breathed a sigh of relief. They weren't going to cut him off.

Deckard's control was shaky and the first batter hit a bouncer to Scrapper's right, forcing him to chase after it and snag it backhanded. As he brought his glove down, he dropped the ball into his right hand, drew back, and fired to Fuller at first for the out. It wasn't a spectacular play. It was just good, solid baseball.

When the next batter, a lefty, came up, everyone shifted slightly to the right. With a two-and-oh count, the batter connected, sending a hard line drive between Garrison and Perez. The shortstop leaped for it, stretching up to get it on the fly.

*Nice catch*, thought Scrapper, knowing that he couldn't have reached the ball if it had come his way. He didn't have Garrison's height or long arms.

He got his first turn at bat in the second inning with one out and a man on first. Scrapper looked at Cravens, expecting the signal for a sacrifice bunt, and when he didn't get it, he tensed for a hard swing, brought his bat around on the first pitch, heard the crack of wood and took off for first, rounding the base and trotting back as the ball landed between right and center field.

Vancouver's next batter hit into shallow left field, forcing the lead runner to hold up on third but loading the bases.

Too excited to stand still, Scrapper danced away from the bag and back again, ready to sprint.

Then the Sox's fifth batter fouled three off before popping up to the first baseman. Deckard stepped to the plate. *A little hit*, thought Scrapper, hopping from one foot to another. *That's all we*

*need. One little hit. You'll get an RBI and we'll be
back to the top of the lineup.*

Deckard judged the first two pitches and let
them go by for a two-and-oh count. On the next
two he swung and missed.

Scrapper shouted, "Go, man go! Do it!"

The Sox pitcher tried but tipped the ball into
the catcher's mitt, retiring the side with three on.

"No sweat, Deck." Scrapper slapped Deckard's
shoulder in the dugout and picked up his glove.
"We'll get 'em next time."

The infield had no plays in the third, but
Scrapper was poised to go right or left each time
the pitcher wound up. It wasn't until the fourth
that the action started.

With one out, a Mariner hit a bullet bouncer to
the right of second base. Scrapper started for it,
saw Garrison running in, and hopped aside as the
shortstop trapped the ball on his knees. Scrambling to his feet, Garrison shot to first. It was a
close play but the ump called the runner out.

"Nice recovery," said Scrapper, hustling back to
the gap.

The next man got on base and Scrapper moved
closer to second. Then Garrison fielded a slow
hopper, throwing to Scrapper on the run.

Scraps took it, saw the base runner sliding in
with feet raised, jumped over him, and threw to
first for the double play.

As they ran off the field, Garrison grinned
sideways and said, "You could have hurt yourself
out there. Nice play."

"Thanks," mumbled Scrapper. He knew he was
taking a chance, that the runner could have

cleated him, but if he had dodged out of the path he wouldn't have made the extra out.

While Calgary's pitcher took time to loosen up, Cravens paced back and forth in the dugout. "So far we're holding our own, but that isn't good enough. Now let's get out there and get some hits, score some runs. Hargis . . . up!"

Ray ran out, dug in, and sent a line drive down the right field line. The next two men flied out— one on a foul to the third baseman, the other on a sweeping pop-up to center field.

Scrapper stepped to the plate with two outs.

"Come on, Mitch!" yelled Ray, taking a short leadoff.

Scrapper fouled two into the stands before laying one on. He knew it was a solid hit but he didn't know *how* solid until his teammates yelled and rushed out of the dugout as the ball dropped over the left field fence.

*My first home run in pro ball!* thought Scrapper, racing around the baselines so fast that his cap flew off as he rounded third and headed for home, where the other players waited to congratulate him.

"What's the rush?" asked Fuller, grinning. "You ran so fast you lost your hat."

"I did?" Scrapper reached up, felt the top of his head, and laughed. "Not used to it, man. I'm not a home run hitter."

"Batter up!" called the ump, jerking his thumb toward the plate and sending the White Sox back to their dugout.

Everyone but Scrapper sat. Unable to settle down, he paced back and forth.

Garrison winked at Perez and moved over to

make room for Scrapper. "Sit down, Mitchell, before you burn out."

"Can't." Scrapper pounded his right fist into his left palm. "My motor's running!"

Cravens stood back against the wall and watched with a smile as his team responded to Scrapper's enthusiasm with friendly laughter and jibes. What the team needed was spirit and it looked like the second baseman just might be the one to get them going.

Perez caught a line drive in the eighth, ending a scoring threat, and the Sox ran to the locker room with a 2–1 victory.


"Motor still running, Mitchell?" asked Garrison as they climbed out of a van in front of the motel.

"You got it!" Scrapper hopped over the curb and punched his arm forward at the empty air. The other players laughed.

*It feels food to be part of a team again*, thought Scrapper.

# NINE

David was about to agree to another beach get-together when Sisko stuck his head around the corner.

"Green! In here!"

Vint rolled his eyes toward the ceiling. "Good luck," he said as David rose and followed the coach to his office.

"Close the door," said Sisko, sitting behind his desk and picking up a newspaper. "You *have* seen this, haven't you?"

"No, sir."

Sisko handed the paper across the desk and rested his chin on his hands while David read.

The headline, "Wonder Boy Scalps Braves," was circled in red. Below it was a two-column account of the previous day's game. More than half of the space was devoted to David. The phrases "brilliant defense," "majestic home runs," "precision play," and "Pawtucket's Canseco" were underlined.

The more David read, the worse he felt. No wonder the fans had turned out to see him. They expected a tiger, and he had let them down. Worse, he had let the team down.

Silently, he handed the paper back.

"What do you suppose they'll say about you after today's game?" Sisko leaned back and fixed David with a hostile glare.

DT swallowed, found his voice, and said, "Nothing good. There isn't much good to say."

"You got that right!" Sisko slammed his fist on his desk, scattering papers right and left. Then he stood up and growled, "If I were you, I'd think twice before I stayed out all night again."

David's eyes widened in surprise.

"There isn't much goes on around here that I don't know about, Green. But it's not my place to baby-sit you guys. You've got two choices. You can work hard and make something of yourself or you can play around and have a good time until you get sent back down—which won't be very long from now if you keep playing like you did today. Do I make myself clear?"

"Yes, sir."

Sisko dismissed him with a wave of his hand.

Except for Vint, the locker room was empty. "You okay?" he asked.

"Yeah, sure. But I think I'll skip the beach."

"You weren't grounded, were you?" Before David could answer, Bobby rushed ahead. "Everyone has a bad day once in a while."

"Especially if they stay up all night. I thought I could wing it, but I couldn't."

"You didn't sleep at all?" asked Bobby, astonished.

"Not on the beach. Hey, aren't you going with the others?" asked David, finally noticing that everyone else had cleared out.

"They're going to pick me up at the motel. I wanted to make sure you were all right before I left."

"You better move then," said David. "I'm okay. All I need is about twelve hours of sack time."

"You got it. I'll be real quiet when I come in."

Vint sprinted for the door and was gone before David could get his cleats off.

In spite of his claim that he was okay, David had a hard time going to sleep. He was worried. He knew Sisko was right. He'd blown one game. If he blew another, he might get a one-way ticket home.

At 7:00 the next morning, he dressed quietly, slipped out of the room, bought a newspaper at the adjoining restaurant, and slid into a booth.

*Might as well get it over with*, he thought, turning to the sports page while he waited for the waitress to take his order. When he saw the headline, his stomach dropped. It was worse than he expected.

"No Wonder, This Boy" jumped out at him with the subheading, "Green lives up to his name!" The reporter, Tom Reed, went on to say that his praise of David Green was an error but a minor one compared to the errors made by the Sox center fielder. His closing paragraph described David as a baseball freak who is "all show" one game and "no go" from then on.

By the time he finished reading the article, David was too angry to finish his breakfast. *A freak, am I?* he thought. *Not this player, Reed. And I'll prove it. Just watch me!*

David was on the field hitting fungoes when the rest of the team came out. Sisko watched his center fielder throw ball after ball up into the air and slug them as they came back down. Finally, he called everyone together.

"Paige, Cummins, Hitchell, warm up," he said to his pitchers. "Teague, Barber, and Williams will catch you. The rest, pick up those balls—and make sure you get 'em all. They're a hazard."

David, along with Vint, Whitehall, and Valdez ran out, scooped up the balls David had hit, and threw them back to Wychinski, who had a hard time keeping up with them.

"Battling practice!" barked Sisko when the field was clear. "Fifteen pitches to everyone. Try," he pleaded sourly, "to hit at least five of them. Cummins, on the mound. You'll start tomorrow night so don't overdo it. But don't lob them in, either."

Teague, first in the lineup, stepped into the batting cage while his teammates took their positions. He missed the first two pitches before connecting on the third and fourth, sending both to third base.

"Easy outs," yelled Sisko. "You're swinging too quick. *Watch* the ball!"

Teague tried but still managed to hit only four more. Barber and Whitehall did no better. While they bounced the ball around the infield, David did some deep knee bends, then leaned forward and stretched from side to side. He felt good—loose, limber, and ready.

Sisko pulled Cummins and put in Hitchell, the number two pitcher. Williams ran out to take center field when David headed for the cage.

Tapping the plate with his bat, he drew back and waited for the first pitch, smashing it past Wychinski at short. The next, a high fly, dropped in between center and right.

It was Vint who started counting after David's sixth straight hit. "Seven!" he yelled when his roommate barrelled one over the right field fence. Another crack of the bat. Everyone but Sisko joined in with "Eight!" then "Nine!"

"Change pitchers!" The coach called in left-hander Paige. "Bear down," he instructed quietly, "and give him your best."

Paige led off with a sidearm pitch— left-hander to left-hander. David stepped into it and caught the ball on the end of his bat for a liner off the center field fence.

"Ten!" roared his teammates.

Paige tried a sinker but David got under it, lifting it over the left fielder's head and into the stands.

"Eleven!"

"*Way* to go!"

"Whoo-oo-ee!"

"That's all, Green!" yelled Sisko, jerking his thumb over his shoulder. "Take the field."

Both Whitehall and Vint trotted over to center field. "Nice goin'," said Whitehall. "Wish he'd uh let you go on, though, at least until you missed one."

"You kiddin'?" asked Vint. "You wanta be here all night?"

"Luck," protested David. "They weren't pitchin' all that tight." But he did have a hard time keeping a straight face. He was on a high and he felt like shouting.

"Better split," he warned. "Wychinski's up and he hits the long ball."

After practice Sisko came into the locker room and read off each player's stats from his clipboard. His comments were varied. "Teague, keep your eye on the ball; Barber, don't crowd the plate; Whitehall, choke up. You're swinging too late. Vint, try a lighter bat. The rest of you—stay sharp! That's it."

"Lookin' good, DT," said Williams after Sisko left. "The man had nothing to say."

"Yeah," agreed Valdez. "If I could hit like DT, I wouldn't be eighth in the lineup."

"Thanks," groaned Paige, who batted ninth.

"Pitchers aren't supposed to hit," said Barber. "All you gotta do is strike out everyone."

"Easier said than done." Paige motioned toward David. "Just cross your fingers he doesn't get traded."

"Yeah," put in Vint. "At least not 'til we knock off the Mets. They think *they're* good! They haven't seen anything yet."

David wasn't so sure. Batting against the Sox pitchers, whose style he knew, was one thing. Batting against an unknown was something else.

"Move it! Move it!" ordered Sisko, waving everyone off when the bus stopped at Tidewater. "We're late. You got ten minutes to get on the field. Let's get some work in before anyone's here to watch."

Most of the players were still tucking in shirt-tails when they ran out of the tunnel.

"Here's the lineup," said Sisko as they gathered around him. "Teague, Barber, Whitehall, Green . . ."

David's eyes widened. The cleanup spot!

"All right!" said Vint, elbowing David gently in the ribs.

"I got a good feelin' about tonight," DT said as Teague stepped up to the plate. "It's gonna be a track meet with us doin' all the runnin'."

Teague, after taking two, golf-balled one into deep center for a two-bagger. Barber popped up into right, but Whitehall struck out.

"Come on, Slugger! Go get 'em!" yelled Vint, as David took his place in the on-deck circle.

After a glance over his shoulder at Teague, the Mets pitcher wound up and hurled a ball high and inside, forcing David to lean away from the pitch. On the next one, DT had to suck in his stomach as the ball caught the front of his shirt—two and oh. Backing out of the box, he swung his bat around like a windmill, stepped back in, tapped the plate, and got set.

Leaning forward, the Mets pitcher studied David, waited for the catcher's signal, stretched his arms up, drew them in close to his chest, and putting everything he had into it, hurled a curve ball to the outside corner.

David laid into it, met the ball a fraction of a second before it got to the plate, and blasted it out of the ball park.

"Two up!" yelled Barber, waiting at the plate as both Teague and DT scored.

"Way to start!" called Vint with a thumbs-up sign.

DT's home run got everyone pumped up. Vint singled into right, Williams skipped one past the second baseman and into center field, taking first as Vint raced around to third. Wychinski popped one over the shortstop's head and Vint raced for home.

"Wha'd I tell ya?" DT yelled, jumping down into the dugout. "A track meet!"

"We got a long way to go yet," warned Sisko. "And they've got more power hitters than we have."

Valdez ended the inning with a pop foul, and the Sox took the field with a three-run lead in the top of the first.

All the action was in the outfield where Whitehall chased down a fly ball, catching it on the run, and David snagged a line drive for the second out. Valdez, playing deep at second, backed up for another fly, signaled for the catch and watched as the ball dropped into his glove to retire the side with no runs, no hits, and no errors.

"How's that?" crowed Williams. "Three up and three down!"

"Game's not over yet, Williams," warned Sisko.

It was in the bottom of the third. Cummins tagged the lead-off batter on the hand, sending him to first. The next two batters singled to load the bases. Sisko went out to the mound and talked to Cummins but left him in.

The Mets' fourth batter stepped up, and after slicing one to the right, out of play, lined into dead center. David took off, charging the ball, as the runner left third.

Not stopping his forward motion, DT drew back and fired straight to Williams, who scooped up the ball and tagged the runner before he could touch home plate. One down but the bases were still loaded.

"Nice throw!" yelled Vint across the outfield. "I probably woulda gone for first."

David grinned at him and backed up, ready for the next shot. It never came. Cummins, using every pitch he knew, struck out the side, and the home team fans, who a minute before had been rooting wildly, fell silent.

Hoping for another home run, David got under the ball too much, lifted it too high, and the left fielder drifted over for the out.

"Don't try so hard," said Sisko when David stepped down into the dugout.

David nodded, took the coach's advice, forgot about home runs, and concentrated on hitting the ball. He came up with a single and a double, driving in two more runs to end the game with a 5–0 win for the Sox.

It felt great to be back in form—three for four. He decided to call home with the good news. It was late but he was sure his mom would still be up. He could almost see her setting the kitchen in order after getting everyone to bed. The phone was only a step away—close enough for her to reach it before the jangling disturbed anyone.

# TEN

The trip from Albuquerque to Vancouver was long and tiring. Roberto relaxed in the reclining seat of the small charter flight, but he was too wound up to get any sleep. He could hardly wait to see Scrapper.

As soon as they reached their motel and got settled in, he reached into his shirt pocket and took out the picture postcard he had received only two days before. There was nothing written on the back except, "Magic—752–9803. On the double!" followed by an illegible scribble.

As the phone rang on the other end of the line, Roberto smiled. Letters had never been Scrapper's strong point. He was too hyper to sit long enough to write down his thoughts.

"Scraps?" Roberto recognized his friend's voice immediately.

"Magic! What took you so long? I've been hogging the phone for the last two hours."

"We just got here. Had a detour. It slowed us down so much that Capella's called off our night practice."

"Great! I'll be right over. Don't go . . ."

Afraid that Scrapper was about to hang up, Roberto interrupted, "Don't you want to know where I am?"

"Guess that would help," admitted Scrapper with a laugh.

"Sleep-Rite Motel. Room sixty-five. Route . . ."

"I know where it is. See ya!"

Roberto took a quick shower and was pulling on his shirt when he heard the squeal of brakes outside, followed by a rapid pounding on the door before Scrapper burst into the room, grinning from ear to ear. Balling up his fist, he gave Roberto the old team salute: a slap on the elbow.

"Watch it," said Magic, trying to sound stern. "That's my pitchin' arm."

"It is?" asked Scrapper with wide-eyed innocence before stepping back to get a better look at Magic. "You've grown," he accused.

"Nah. You've shrunk."

Scrapper pulled himself up to his full five feet seven inches. "We Mitchells never shrink—from anything. Let's go somewhere, get some food, and talk. I borrowed my roommate's car."

"What time's curfew?" he asked as they pulled away from the motel.

"Ten o'clock. Early practice tomorrow."

"You pitchin'?"

"Is the sky blue?"

Scrapper groaned before flashing a sideways grin. "Too bad, ole buddy. I always did hate to see you lose." He took his hands from the wheel and, fists clenched, drew his arms back over his right shoulder.

"Hey, watch it!" warned Roberto as the car swerved toward the center line.

"Not to worry. The Scrapper has the reflexes of a cat." Mitchell pulled the car back into line as Roberto leaned back with a happy sigh.

He had missed Scrapper; missed his bragging, his cocky assurance, his quick wit. But most of all, he had missed his friendship.

Instead of going into a restaurant to eat, they stopped at a drive-in, ordered curb service, and stayed in the car.

"If we go in anywhere, I'll be mobbed by admiring fans," stated Scrapper before bursting into a laugh.

"I know what you mean," said Roberto, keeping a straight face. "But if you expect any of those fans to buy your endorsements, you'd better do something about that chicken scratch you call a signature. Who wants a bat with nothing but a scribble on it?"

"Everyone! I can see it now," said Scrapper. "Kids lined up around the block to buy Scrapper Mitchell bats, gloves, uniforms, balls."

"No one endorses baseballs."

"*I* will. And if you stick by me, I'll let *you* do a few, too."

After they finished their baskets of fried chicken and chips, they talked about home, their days at Rosemont High, and Coach LaRusso, both agreeing that the only thing that kept the evening from being a perfect one was the absence of DT.

"He's doin' okay, though," said Scrapper. "Gettin' a lot o' ink."

Roberto agreed, adding, "I'll bet he gets called to Boston before the year's out."

"Before you and me?" asked Scrapper with wide-eyed disbelief.

"Well, before me, anyhow." Then Roberto told Scrapper about beaning Billy Mills.

"You had a slump after that, didn't you?"

"More like a nose dive," admitted Roberto. He went on to describe the next two times he had had to pitch. It was good to be able to talk to someone about it—someone who understood him— someone like Scrapper.

Scraps admitted that he had gotten off on the wrong foot, too, because of his big mouth, but that he was learning to curb his temper and was getting along better than ever.


Roberto was always nervous before a game and felt especially uptight about this one. So he took longer than usual to warm up and by the time he went to the mound, he was relaxed and knew he could face his friend as easily as he faced any other ballplayer.

The White Sox's first batter went down on three fast balls, two inside and one out. Scrapper stepped to the plate. Roberto wound up and sent a split-fingered sidearm curve.

Scrapper saw the ball heading straight for him but he held his ground. He knew it would curve in and it did. He laid down a perfect bunt, easily beating it out to first.

But Roberto knew Scrapper. He would try to steal the first chance he got. In front of the rubber now for a stretch pitch instead of a full windup, he glanced toward first. Scraps had taken a lead but he was poised to scurry back to first if he had to.

Magic shot one in over the outside corner for strike one. Scrapper went back to first and tagged up before taking another lead, a longer one.

When Roberto did fire to first, Scrapper had to dive, his hand touching the bag a split second before the first baseman caught the throw. Scrambling to his feet, he brushed dust from the front of his uniform and edged back down the base line. Roberto tugged at the neck of his uniform—a signal for Jim to watch for a steal.

When Jim nodded, Roberto hurled a shoulder-high fastball. Scraps took off for second. The batter swung under the ball and Roberto stepped out of the line of fire. Jim, overanxious and a little off balance, missed his target, pulling the second baseman off the bag. Scrapper slid in safe.

Glancing over his right shoulder at Mitchell, Roberto wound up and delivered another hard ball, low and inside. Jim was on his feet immediately, ready for a throw to third, but Scrapper held his ground. There was only one out and he was in scoring position. He had plenty of time.

Roberto scraped at the dirt in front of the rubber with his toe, filling in the divot. His follow-through hadn't been as smooth as he liked on that last pitch. Once again he stepped back off the mound and this time he motioned for the second and third basemen to move in. Maybe they couldn't catch Scrapper off base but they might be able to catch him between bases if he attempted another steal.

Facing the batter again, he sent a curve ball down the pike for an infield out. Scrapper stayed on second. After turning the ball over and over in his hand, Roberto called for a new one, threw the old ball in, and waited while the ump reached into his pocket.

The fourth man up was a slugger. Roberto leaned forward, took his time, then straightened up and fired a sinker, too low, for ball one. One glance back at Scrapper told him what he needed to know. His friend had stayed close to second because he expected his own teammate to blast one.

After that, Roberto was careful not to give the batter anything close to a home run pitch. When he reached a full count, he called for a tongue depresser and cleaned the dirt out from between his cleats. Then he sent one in low. The batter, frustrated by the delay, tried to golfball it and went down swinging.

Scrapper detoured toward the mound on his way to the Sox dugout and called, "Nice pitchin'." Then, with an impish grin, "Next time, Magic."

"No way, Scraps," Roberto said.

The next two innings flew by with each team scoring two runs. Roberto watched from the sidelines as Scrapper made two outstanding plays.

"Your friend's pretty good," said Packard.

"One of the best," agreed Roberto with a smile as he took off his jacket and went to kneel in the on-deck circle. It was his first time at bat in the game and he was psyched.

Davis hit a ground ball between first and second. Scraps made a dive for it but it bounced over his glove and rolled into the outfield for a hit.

Roberto stepped up to the plate. He expected the first pitch to be in there and it was, but he swung too late. The next he let go by for the oh-and-two count. Studying the pitcher, he saw the sidearm pitch coming and caught it on the end of his bat, sending it into left field.

With no outs and the top of the batting order coming up, the Dodgers had a rally going.

At the top of the order, the next batter hit a line drive into the shortstop's glove. The second man flied out to center field. Two down. The White Sox pitcher relaxed, let up too much on his next pitch, and Packard blasted one into deep left field.

Scrapper ran in to cover second as Roberto raced for the bag and Davis held up on third.

"Pitchers aren't supposed to get hits," grumbled Scrapper.

"I've been practicing," said Roberto.

"Well, do your practicing on someone else, Magic. Make me look good. I deserve it."

Roberto laughed. "What for? Stealing a base on me?"

Scrapper drifted off the bag in time to field a chopper and throw the runner out at first, ending the Dodgers' scoring threat.

Once again, Roberto faced his friend. He watched for a bunt, but instead Scrapper jumped on the first pitch, sending it straight back. Roberto sidestepped and caught the ball before it could streak past him for the first out. Scrapper took off his helmet and banged it against his leg, grumbling.

The next batter stepped to the plate, swinging his bat back and forth in wide arcs before digging in. Roberto concentrated on low pitches, getting one over the plate and two outside. On the fourth pitch, the man swung, connecting and zinging it back toward the mound.

This time Roberto wasn't quick enough. The ball crashed into his right toe with the force of a rocket and his leg collapsed. He dropped to his knees.

Davis reached him seconds before Capella. By the time Cap got there, Roberto was back on his feet, his weight centered on his left leg.

"It's okay," he said. But when he tried to stand, a sharp pain shot up to his knee.

Capella and Davis helped him off the field and Parsons went in to finish the game. Scrapper started to run across the field but was called back by his own coach.

The Dodgers' trainer removed Roberto's shoe and applied ice packs to his foot. "I don't think it's broken," he said, "but we'd better have an X ray to be sure. That was a pretty good hit."

With an ice pack wrapped around his toe, Roberto watched his team go down 4–2. After the last out, Scrapper ran to the Dodger dugout.

"How bad is it, Magic?" he asked, squatting down and gently removing the ice. He winced when he saw Magic's swollen and discolored toe.

"Not bad. Better than getting hit in the head." Roberto tried to sound offhand but there was an edge to his voice.

"Not for a pitcher, it isn't." Scrapper looked up at his friend seriously. He knew they were both thinking the same thing, that it was a broken toe that had ended Dizzy Dean's brilliant pitching career.

"They'll take you to St. Joseph's. I'll see you there, Magic. Don't go 'way."

Roberto nodded and grinned but he was more worried than he let on. His teammates had tried to reassure him, but when he saw Cap frown and shake his head, his doubts returned.

# ELEVEN

Thinking only of Roberto and afraid that his friend's baseball career might be over, Scrapper showered and dressed in record time.

"Mitch!" yelled Ray, tossing his keys over as Scraps dashed for the locker-room door. "Take my car. I'll catch a ride."

"Thanks!" Scrapper ran out of the ball park, climbed into Ray's car, and headed downtown to St. Joseph's Hospital.

"Roberto Ramirez," he said to the young woman at the main desk of the hospital. "Where is he?"

The woman punched Roberto's name in on a computer and shook her head. "No Ramirez here," she said.

"Gotta be! He was hurt in tonight's game. Look again."

"Maybe he was brought in to Emergency. That wouldn't be on my list yet. You might try there," she suggested with a kind smile.

"Where is it?"

"Down that hall"—she gestured to her right—
"and—"

Scrapper didn't wait for her to finish. He took
off.

". . . to your left," she called after him.

When he reached the emergency waiting room,
he found the Dodgers' trainer, Carter, sitting patiently and leafing through a magazine.

"How's Ramirez?"

"He's still inside," said Carter, looking up as he
flipped another page. "Might as well sit down. It
could take a while."

Scrapper sat on the edge of one of the plastic
chairs, his fingers drumming nervously on his
knees. After five minutes had passed, he got up,
opened the door to the medical offices, and
peeked in.

On both sides were curtains enclosing treating
rooms. Letting the door swish shut behind him, he
edged forward until he could see around and into
the first area. It was empty. On tiptoes, he worked
his way down the aisle until he found Roberto
sitting on the edge of a gurney, his feet resting on
a high stool.

"You shouldn't be in here," Magic said, smiling.

"I know. Don't tell anyone." Scrapper grinned
but kept his voice low. "So what's the damage?"

"Noth . . ."

"Here we are." A white-coated man of about
forty, with closely clipped brown hair and a
serious expression, strode around the end of the
curtain. When he saw Scrapper, he looked from
one boy to the other and frowned.

"You obviously aren't brothers. Friends are supposed to wait outside."

"Yes, sir," said Scrapper, not budging.

The doctor sighed, but went on. "Nothing broken. Just a bad sprain. The swelling will go down in a week or so. In the meantime, don't put any weight on that foot. You're lucky. Most pitchers who get hit like you did wind up with a broken bone."

"The ball hit my pitching toe," explained Roberto. "I guess the metal plate took most of the beating."

"Mm-mm. It's still best to stay off of it for a few days. I sent one of the aides for crutches so wait here until she gets back. *You* . . ." he frowned again at Scrapper.

"I know—wait outside." Scrapper grinned, winked at Roberto, and squeezed past the doctor. But he didn't leave the hospital until Magic was released, helped into a Dodger van, and headed back to his room.


"How's your friend?" asked Packard that night as the Sox were dressing for the night game.

"Gonna be okay. Hey, you guys don't know how lucky we are. If Magic had pitched that whole game, we'd have lost."

"What's with you bozos from—Roseweed, is it?—are you *all* superstars?" asked Perez, reaching for his socks.

"Rose*mont*," corrected Scraper, slipping one arm into his shirt. "We're not *all* superstars. Just Magic Ramirez, DT Green, and . . . me, of course," he added with a grin.

Perez groaned, rolled up his sock, and threw it at Scrapper, who couldn't get his arm through his shirt in time to catch it.

"Hey," cried Scraps, ducking. "I wasn't ready."

"I thought you were always ready," teased Packard.

"I am," boasted Scraps. He picked up the sock and threw it back. "That's why my friends call me 'Scrapper.'"

"'Scrapper'?" said Garrison, making a face. "I can believe that! You sure started out like a first-class geek."

"Yeah," yelled a teammate.

"Right on!"

"Just for the first game," said Scrap, reaching into his locker for his cap. "But," he continued with an impish grin, "like the fine player that I am, I got right back up and won you over." Then he swept off his cap and bowed, covering his head with one arm to fend off the avalanche of towels he knew would be coming his way.

More hoots and hollers followed, stopping only when Cravens stepped into the room and asked what was going on.

"Just a little locker-room humor, Coach," said Scrapper, straightening up.

"Well, save some of that energy for the game." Cravens suppressed a smile. "The Dodgers will be starting a new pitcher tonight, one they just brought up so we don't know much about him. Scouting reports are pretty thin. Name's Stillman. Mean anything to anyone?"

Everyone shook his head.

"Okay. Here's the plan. The best way to shake up a new pitcher is to get some hits right away—

before he has a chance to gain much confidence. That's why I'm moving Mitchell up to the starting post. Everyone else will drop down one in the batting order. Any questions?"

Cravens glanced around the room at the silent players and then came back to Scrapper. "When you get on base, Mitchell, take second. The sooner we get a man in scoring position, the better. Okay. Let's go!"

The Dodgers opened the game with a single and a triple, then lost their rally quickly. The next batter struck out, and a double play to second after a pop-out to the catcher put the visitors in the field.

Practicing his swings, Glen gave Magic the "hi" sign when he spotted him in the Dodger dugout.

Shifting his attention, Scrapper watched Stillman closely as the pitcher warmed up. He wasn't throwing anything very hard but that didn't mean he couldn't. When the umpire called "Batter up!" Scraps stepped to the plate, crouched slightly, and let the first pitch go by for a ball. When the second ball came in he thought, *Don't walk me, Stillman, don't walk me.*

Stillman didn't. He sent a fastball over the plate and Scrapper jumped on it, sending it down the right field line. Keeping his eye on the fielder, who raced after the fair ball, Scraps rounded first without even slowing down, dug in, and headed for second, diving into the base in a cloud of dust and stretching a single into a double.

Vancouver's fans cheered the extra effort. They were hungry for another victory.

Scrapper took a long lead and when he saw a high fly coming down to the right fielder for an easy out, he ran back to second, tagged up, and waited until the opposing player caught the ball. Then he sprinted for third, sliding in safely ahead of the throw.

When the next man grounded out to short, Scrapper got antsy. "Come on, Hargis!" he yelled. "Keep us goin'!"

Ray bounced one off the center field wall for a stand-up double and Scrapper raced for home. Crossing the plate at top speed, he ran straight into the outstretched hands of his teammates in the dugout.

"Don't you ever slow down?" drawled Perez when Scraps flopped down beside him.

"Slow down, you get caught, man."

Perez shook his head but when he left the dugout for the on-deck circle, he ran. Scrapper's enthusiasm was catching. And when he got to the plate, with two on, two outs and a full count, he popped one over the second baseman's head, allowing Hargis to score and giving the Sox a two-run lead.

After that Stillman got into stride, retiring the side. He allowed no runs in the next two innings while the Dodgers tied it up in the top of the fourth.

Scrapper hit one through the hole in the fourth and stole second, but was left on base as the Dodger outfielders tightened their defense and closed the inning.

As he ran back to the dugout for his glove, he gave Deckard the high sign and paused at the mound just long enough to say, "Bear down, Deck. You can do it. Let's show those Dodgers what a real team looks like!"

Deckard held the Dodgers off through the eighth inning, and both teams went into the ninth with two runs. The score was still tied. Hargis led off the bottom of the inning with a double to left field and advanced to third on Perez's single. With two men in scoring position and no outs, the fans began to roar.

"Go! Go!"

"Come on, Sox!"

Scrapper sat on the edge of his seat in the dugout, his toes impatiently tapping to the rhythm of the crowd.

The next man up hit straight to the second baseman, who tagged up, glanced long enough toward Hargis to hold him on third, and threw to first for the double play.

Scrapper got to his feet and began to pace back and forth. They needed a run. They needed it bad. *Down the first base line*, he thought, crossing his fingers as the next Sox batter went to the plate. *That'll give Hargis enough time to score.*

But the batter bounced one to the shortstop, loading the bases but forcing Hargis to hold up.

"Come on, Garrison!" yelled Scrapper, leaning out of the dugout. "Blast it!"

The fans behind the third base line heard him and took up the cry. "Blast it! Blast it!" they shouted, standing and waving their caps.

Garrison took one for a strike but that didn't slow the fans down. It only worked them into more of a frenzy. He tried for a home run, putting everything he had into a swing that spun him around as the ball whizzed past him for strike two.

Scrapper tried to relax but he couldn't. When the next pitch went by for a ball, he took off his cap and began to wring it. By the time Garrison reached a full count, he had crushed the visor.

*This is it*, thought Scraps, as Stillman wound up and let go with a fastball down the middle.

Garrison hopped on it, coming around late, but knocking it into center field while Hargis ran home to put the Sox ahead.

Stillman's shoulders drooped and he took longer to get set for the Sox's next batter—Deckard.

Scrapper knelt in the dugout as the Sox pitcher took his turn at bat, popping out to the catcher, and leaving three on.

"No sweat! We got the lead! Let's hold 'em!" cried Scraps as he ran out to second.

Deckard was beginning to tire and the first two Dodger batters got on base with clean singles.

When the third batter, a left-hander, came to the plate, Scraps motioned for the first baseman to cover the hole while he moved slightly toward Garrison, closing the gap between second and third.

After fouling off two pitches, the Dodger batter connected with a speeding line drive. Scrapper reached out and gloved it backhanded, spun around to touch second, doubling out the runner already on his way to third, then fired to first to end the game with a triple play.

The fans, who had held their breath while the Dodgers put two on with no outs, rose to their feet, yelling and throwing empty paper cups in the air. Some of them had seen triple plays in the majors but none had seen one on their home field.

"Good job, Mi—Scrapper!" called Garrison as he and Scrapper ran off the field.

Suddenly Mitchell was surrounded by team-mates.

"What a play!"

"Outta sight!"

"Smooth move!"

"Hey, man, nothin' to it," Scrapper hung his head and then, with a sidelong wink at Hargis, said, "No big deal, guys. I can walk to the locker room. You don't have to carry me."

"Hoo!" cried someone at the rear of the circle. He took off his hat and threw it at Scraps. His teammates followed with more "Hoo's" and a cascade of caps, which Scraps fended off with a laugh and upraised arms.


That night Scrapper went to Magic's room where they spent the rest of the night talking about baseball. At 11:00 they turned on the sports roundup.

The Boston Red Sox had lost another game, the third in a row. "Looks like the Sox's long-ball hitters are in a slump," said the announcer. "Maybe they need a little new life."

Scrapper and Magic looked at each other, their eyes shining, and said, "DT" at the same time.

"Here's a bit of bad luck, fans," continued the sportscaster. "Chicago White Sox second base-man, Al Gardino, in an attempt to chase down a fly ball, crashed into the stands and broke his right leg. Looks like he'll be out for the rest of the season."

Magic looked at his friend, who sat with his eyes closed, barely breathing. "You're going up," he predicted.

But Scrapper shook his head.

"After tonight's game they can't pass you over," argued Magic.

More than anything, Scrapper wanted to get the call, but he continued to shake his head, afraid to hope, afraid he *might* be passed over.

# TWELVE

After the phone rang six times, David knew something was wrong. It was 10:00 P.M. in Chicago. Where was everyone?

Finally, his little brother answered.

"Ned!" said DT. "What are you still doin' up? Where's Mom?"

"Dave?" Ned's voice rose with excitement.

"Who else at this time of night? Let me talk to Mom."

"Hit any more home runs?" asked Ned, reluctant to give up the phone.

"Got one today," said David patiently. "Went three for four. Mom, Ned, Mom. Let me talk to her."

"Okay. M-o-m-m-m!" Ned shrieked so loud that David flinched and held the receiver away, almost missing his brother yelling, "It's Dave. Are you gonna tell him?"

"Sh-sh," shushed his mother before taking the phone. "David!" she exclaimed. "How are you?"

"I'm okay, Mom," said DT, forgetting about his reason for calling. "Why is Ned still up? What's wrong?"

"Wrong? Nothing's wrong. Everyone's fine. Now tell me how *you're* doing."

"Don't try to change the subject, Mom," insisted DT. "I heard what Ned said."

Mrs. Green took a deep breath and let it out slowly. "It's nothing, David. Nothing unusual, that is. Ned flunked a math test and he didn't want you to know."

"M-o-m-m-m!" Ned's small voice protested faintly through the wire.

David stared at the receiver. Ned, the brightest of his younger brothers and sisters, was a whiz at math. And the boy's objection told him that whatever the problem was, it wasn't Ned's math grades.

*Laurie?* wondered David. *Has she taken off again?*

"How's Laurie?" he asked guardedly.

"Just fine," said Mrs. Green. "Prettier than ever. She's watching TV—one of her favorite shows. Want me to call her?"

"No," said David hurriedly, "no need to interrupt." He could picture his sister, who had enough temper for the whole family, flouncing to the phone, irritated at missing "the best part."

David thought he heard a sigh of relief before his mother repeated that everyone was all right. David told her about his terrific run of luck, then his money ran out. He barely had time to say good-bye.

"Troubles?" asked Vint after David hung up.

"Don't know for sure." David frowned and rubbed his forehead.

"Anything I can do to help?"

"No, thanks. I can't even do anything—not from here at least." He paused. "But there *is* someone back home who . . . Can you lend me some quarters?"

Vint dug into his pocket, came up with a handful of change, and handed it to Green. David picked up the phone and dialed a number he knew almost as well as his mother's.

It rang three times before a sleepy man's voice answered.

"Coach?" David said. No answer. "Could I talk to Coach Tony LaRusso? I know it's late and all, but I really . . ."

"Damn straight it's late. Who is this, anyway?"

"Coach! It's DT Green."

"Well, DT Green," he said, clearing his throat "how's it going? I hear you're knocking the ball all over the park, making Rosemont look good, kid, damn good!"

"Thanks," mumbled David, suddenly uncertain about involving his old high school coach in his own problems.

"What is it, Green?" asked LaRusso gently, sensing the other's hesitation. "And don't tell me you just called to say hello," he added.

"No. No, I didn't." David took a deep breath and plunged ahead. "I need a favor."

"You name it, you got it."

"Check up on my family, would you? See if you can find out what's goin' on? I just talked to Mom and she didn't sound like herself. She *said* everything was okay, but I'm afraid my sister Laurie's in some kind of trouble again.

"Sure. First thing tomorrow morning. I'll get back to you as soon as I know anything. And, DT, try not to worry. If there *is* something wrong, it can't be too serious or your mother would have told you."

"Thanks." David gave him both the Tidewater and Pawtucket numbers and hung up. Just talking to LaRusso made him feel better. If anyone could help him, he could.

Even so, he slept fitfully that night and when LaRusso didn't call back the following morning, he had to struggle in the second game against the Mets, who came back from their defeat with a resounding 6–1 victory over the Sox.

With his mind on his family, David played like a robot with a weak battery. He popped up twice, struck out once, and got only one hit—a liner that slipped past the first baseman. And with a Mets player on first, he made a bad throw, over the second baseman's head, allowing the runner to take second.

*If Paige hadn't struck out the next three batters that man would have scored*, thought David as he ran in.

Sisko said nothing about the wild throw when the game ended and the players plodded silently past him in to the locker room.

"Pack up," he ordered. "Grab some take-outs to eat on the way home. We're starting back in forty-five minutes."

"We'll hear more about this tomorrow," said Vint as he and David changed.

David nodded in agreement.

Back at the motel, David kept his eyes on the phone as he packed, hoping LaRusso would call before they left.

"You comin'?" asked Bobby.

"Yeah, yeah, sure." David took one last long look at the silent phone and followed Vint outside.

"Green!" bellowed Sisko, his voice cutting through the locker room. "Front and center!"

"Uh-oh," mumbled Teague as everyone tried not to look at David.

DT threaded his way through the room. *Another chewing-out*, he thought glumly.

"Phone," said Sisko curtly. "My office. And don't take all day."

LaRusso? David's heart skipped a beat. All morning he had sat in his room at the motel, not even going out to eat, just waiting for the phone to ring.

"Coach?" he asked breathlessly.

"Sorry I took so long to get back to you," said LaRusso, "but I couldn't get hold of your mother right away and then I had to worm the story out of her."

"It's Laurie, isn't it?" David, his knees weak, sank down into Sisko's swivel chair. "What happened?"

"It's a long story but I'll cut it short. Seems Laurie skipped school last week, got caught, was suspended for three days, and wouldn't go back. Said she was going to quit school and get a full-time job at the mall."

David squeezed his eyes shut. "I gotta talk to her. I'll catch the first plane. . . ."

"Hey, hold on!" interrupted LaRusso. "You can't do that. You've got a career to think about. Besides, I've already had a talk with her. I didn't get through to her, though, until I told her that if she didn't straighten up, you *would* come home and she'd ruin your chances of ever making it to the big leagues. That girl has her faults but she thinks a lot of you, Green. Anyhow, she agreed to come back to school."

David felt like an immense weight had been lifted from his shoulders. "Thanks, Coach," he choked out.

"All in a day's work, Slugger. Now get out there and show 'em what Rosemont players are made of!"

"You bet!" David hung up, tossed his cap into the air, and caught it on the run as he raced out of the office, through the empty locker room, and onto the field.

"Bad news?" asked Vint, lingering near the tunnel entrance, waiting apprehensively for David.

"Into the cage, Green." Sisko yelled.

"Tell you about it later," DT shouted as he ran out.

David picked up his favorite bat, a thirty-six-ounce ash Louisville Slugger, took some practice swings, and stepped into the cage. He felt as if he could hit anything. And he did.

No one counted his hits this time but after he belted three into the upper decks, everyone stopped what they were doing and watched.

"Enough!" cried Sisko after David's twelfth straight hit against three different pitchers. "Get in here."

"What's with you, Green?" he asked when David

joined him. "One day you play like a real pro, the next day like an amateur. You're not consistent. And that's the one thing you have to be. The man who can get on base regularly and play the field well is a lot more valuable to a team than someone who bombs every other game. You've got to get your act together or you're going to blow your big chance."

It was a long speech for Sisko and while David nodded his head in agreement, he didn't understand what the coach meant by "blowing his big chance."

That night David and Bobby sat up late watching TV. David told him about Laurie and about Sisko's remarks.

"'Blowing your big chance'?" said Bobby, his eyes shining. "Boston, man, Boston. That's what he meant. They're getting ready to call you up!"

"After the way I've been playing?" asked David doubtfully.

"What else? Sure, you had a couple of bad days but you had some good ones, too. Fantastic home runs, super fielding. Think about it!"

David did think about it. He thought about it long after Bobby had fallen asleep. The Boston Red Sox. Fenway Park. The Green Monster, that high green wall in left field. But first he had to prove himself.

He was still thinking about Boston and Fenway Park the next day when the starting lineups were announced over the P.A. system. As he ran onto the field and turned to face the crowded stands, he scanned the seats behind home plate and along the first-base line, trying to find someone who might be a scout, someone with a note pad. But he saw no one.

When the game started, he pushed everything out of his mind except the contest with the Orioles, who were battling the Sox for second place in the league. It was going to be a tough game.

Baltimore scored two runs in the first inning, while Teague, Barber, and Whitehall failed to get on base.

After holding the Orioles scoreless in the second, David started off the bottom half with a line drive up the alley in left center. Taking a long lead off first, he gauged the pitcher's timing until he saw his chance, sliding safely into second amid a round of applause from Sox fans.

Vint smashed one into right and DT took off, rounding third as the base-line coach swung his arm in a frantic circle and yelled, "Go! Go!"

David crossed the plate standing up to give the Red Sox their first run.

Williams and Wychinski both flied out to end the inning, leaving Vint on second. David grabbed his glove and trotted out to center field.

Then Sox pitcher, Paige, ran into trouble—walking the first man and giving up a double to put a man on second and third.

*All they need to score is a long fly ball,* thought David, playing deep but ready to charge forward if he had to.

With two strikes on him, the Orioles batter lifted one over the infield. David ran in. He caught the ball knee high, rolled it into his right hand, drew back and gunned it home. Williams snapped it up and tagged the incoming runner for a double play.

But they weren't out of trouble yet. There was a man on third.

The next Orioles batter fouled off two, both long balls, before catching one on the end of his bat and powering it into right center.

David raced back, pulled up short of the fence, leaped, and snagged the ball backhanded before it could drop into the first row of the stands.

The fans went wild.

"Great catch, Green!" Wychinski slapped David on the back as they ran into the dugout.

"Some throw!" said Sox catcher Williams, with awe. "I didn't have to move an inch."

Vint winked at David, leaned close, and said, "You're on a roll, man. Bring out that big bat and you've got it made."

David grinned. *If only it were that easy*, he thought.

Valdez led off with a single, followed by Paige with a foul tip for the first out. Teague and Barber both singled to load the bases but Whitehall struggled too hard and struck out again.

With the bases loaded and two outs, David took a deep breath and started forward.

# THIRTEEN

After Scrapper saw Roberto safely on his way, he headed back to the motel.

"What took you so long?" asked Hargis. "Cravens called three times."

"Cravens? What about?" Scrapper's stomach began to do flip-flops. The coach had never called him before. Could Roberto be right? Had the Chicago team sent for him? *No, they wouldn't send for anyone this soon,* he thought. *It must be something else. They have enough utility players to take over second base temporarily, maybe permanently.*

"He didn't say. Not exactly." Hargis bent over and picked up a piece of lint from the floor so Scrapper wouldn't see the smile he couldn't hide.

In two long strides, Scraps crossed the room and picked up the phone. "What do you mean 'not exactly'? What's his number? Was he calling from home?"

"Yeah. He just said to tell you to get yourself out there right away. I'll drive you."

"I can go by myself." Scrapper was halfway across the room when Hargis snapped his fingers. "Darn! I almost forgot. You're supposed to bring your stuff."

"My stuff?" Scrapper's heart began to race.

"Yeah, as in clothes." Ray's face split in a grin. "You're goin' *up*, Scraps!"

"He said that? He said I'm goin' up?"

"Well, no," admitted Ray, "but what else could it be? You sure aren't goin' down, not the way *you* play and with Chicago's second baseman out for the season. . . ."

"Yow-e-e-e!" Scrapper jumped up and slapped the top of the door frame with the palm of his hand. Then he yanked his suitcase out from under his bed, opened dresser drawers, scooped up clothes, and began stuffing them into the case.

"My mom would choke at the way you're packing," said Ray.

"So would mine. But this time, I think she'd forgive me. My jackets," said Scrapper, leaning on the over-filled bag. "They'll never go in here."

"Carry 'em. Here." Ray opened the closet, pulled out Scrapper's coats and slipped a plastic cover over them.

"Ugh! There!" Scraps forced the lid shut and snapped the locks. Then he had a horrible thought. "This *is* for real, isn't it? You wouldn't kid me?"

"No," said Hargis, "it's not a joke and I wouldn't kid you. Those first couple of weeks you were here I might have. But not now."

"I was kind of a pain, wasn't I?"

"A *real* pain. A dipstick! Come on. Let's move."

Scrapper spent the next three hours in a half daze. First there were the instructions from Cravens, then the drive to the airport and the wait for his plane to take off.

Hargis insisted on staying with him. "I may never get the call," he said, "but at least I can say I played and roomed with a major leaguer. And saw him off," he added with a grin.

"Just hang in there," said Scrapper when his flight was called. "And I'll see you in Chicago."

*Chicago*, he thought, as the plane gained altitude. *Chicago! I'm goin' home! In style!*

Then he slapped his forehead with the heel of his hand. *Magic!—I should have called him before I left. And Dad!*

But when the plane taxied into O'Hare at 3:00 A.M. the next day Scrapper knew *he* couldn't wait. Hailing a cab, he went straight home, got out, and stood looking up at the darkened house. Then he climbed the front steps and leaned on the doorbell.

Lights came on. First in his parents' bedroom, then in the upstairs hall, and finally in the foyer. He could see his mother halfway down the stairs, her robe clutched around her, when his father opened the door.

"Glen?" asked Mrs. Mitchell, anxiously.

Joe Mitchell stared at his son and then began to grin.

"You folks wouldn't have a room for the Chicago White Sox second baseman, would you?" He had planned on playing it cool and pretending it was no big deal, but when he saw his father's face light up, he lost it.

"I made it!" he yelled, clasping his father around the neck. "I made it! I report this afternoon!"

"I knew you would, Glen." Joe Mitchell blinked away the moisture in his eyes. "Let me look at you. I knew you would," he repeated. "And they won't be sorry. You're the best."

"Hey, I guess it runs in the family." Scrapper punched his dad lightly with his fist.

"Come on out to the kitchen," said Mrs. Mitchell. "I'll put some coffee on, too."

"No coffee," said Joe. "Caffeine, this boy doesn't need. He's already wound up."

"And *we're* not?" asked Mrs. Mitchell, her eyes shining.

Scrapper stood outside Comiskey Park for a few minutes, letting the butterflies in his stomach settle down. Then he headed for the team gate. He knew all the players by sight but none personally. So when he saw the third baseman coming in behind him, he turned and said, "Hi. I'm Glen Mitchell. Where can I find the manager?"

The Sox infielder stuck out his hand. "Julio Ruiz. Third base. Heard you were comin' up. Welcome aboard. Andrews will be on the field. Follow me."

*So far, so good,* thought Scrapper, vowing to get off on the right foot this time. *No more hot-dogging,* he promised himself.

Rex Andrews looked him up and down. "We've been hearing some good things about you, Mitchell. Suit up and let's see what you can do. We've got time for a little infield practice before the game."

"Hit some bouncers to second," ordered Andrews when Scrapper came back onto the field. "Let him warm up."

Ball after ball came whizzing toward Glen— high bounces, low bounces, line drives, pop-ups, and with each one, Andrews yelled, "First," "Third," or "Home," for the return.

Scrapper was kept too busy to notice the stands filling until the manager called a halt. Then he had a chance to look up and around. He felt dwarfed. He'd been in Comiskey Park before, several times, but not in the middle of the field with thousands of fans surrounding him. Swallowing the lump in his throat, he looked out at the electronic scoreboard in center field and hoped he wouldn't disappoint them.

He did his best not to. His first play was a short hopper that he charged, picking it up and firing to first for the out.

His second was a hard-hit line drive. He jumped and caught it on the tip of his glove.

He didn't bat until the second inning with two on and two outs. His stomach felt hollow. *First-time jitters*, he told himself as the pitcher sent a fastball past him for a call strike.

But the next pitch, a change-up, seemed to hang in the air and he swung too quick. Strike two. He backed out of the box and took some practice swings. Then he took a ball before lifting the next pitch too high, giving the right fielder plenty of time to get under it. Disappointed, he ran to the dugout, picked up his glove, and trotted out to second.

The Sox were trailing 2–1 in the fourth with two men on and one out when Scrapper flagged down a rocket grounder, floated across second, spun, and threw to first for the double play. He began to feel better.

He led off the fifth with a drag bunt down the third base line. Then he stole second and scored on a double to tie the game. He was in top form.

By the time he came to bat in the seventh, the butterflies had flown. Tapping the plate with his bat, he drew back and waited for the first pitch. It came in high and outside for ball one. The next two were also outside. Scrapper looked to the third base coach and got a red light—take one.

Poised, ready to swing, he let the pitch go by for a walk, but was left on base when the Sox failed to score.

*At least I didn't disgrace myself*, he thought when a home run by the Tigers left fielder ended the game with a loss for the Sox.

Scrapper wanted to visit Rosemont and talk to Coach LaRusso but it was another week before he had the chance. By that time he knew he was in solid with the Chicago team. His batting had improved, he'd stolen three more bases, and he'd made two tricky plays that had brought the fans to their feet.

When he did walk into his old locker room after school, LaRusso lifted him off the floor in a bear hug.

"Scrapper! It's about time you came around!"

"Couldn't get away any sooner, Coach," said Scrapper, sneaking a quick look at his old locker—the one he'd slammed his fist into when he was a sophomore and had struck out in the ninth, ruining Rosemont's chance to take the regional.

"The dent is still there," said LaRusso, following Scrapper's gaze.

"Thought you might have had it fixed."

"No way. I use it sometimes to make a point. Tell the boys that if they have the determination this one had, they'll make it." He tapped the locker lightly with his knuckles. "Hey, how about coming out on the field and giving the team some pointers."

Next to Comiskey Park, Rosemont's field looked incredibly small, much smaller than he remembered. One thing hadn't changed, though. The players. They were just as rowdy as his old high school team, jibing and joking with each other as they tossed the ball around the infield.

LaRusso called everyone in. "We got a celebrity with us today," he said, puffing up. "Glen 'Scrapper' Mitchell."

"Mitchell?" asked a short, overweight boy at the rear of the pack. "The new guy with the Sox?"

"Yeah, I saw him play last night."

"Come on! He wouldn't come *here*. Major leaguers don't fool with high school teams."

"It is *so* him," a senior said. "He used to play for Rosemont. I remember he came to visit when I was a sophomore. He's good."

"He's better than good," said LaRusso. "He's the best. So listen up to what he has to say."

"How did you *get* to be so good?" a tall, spare boy asked.

"I practiced," said Scrapper. "*And* practiced and then when I was through, I practiced some more. I also had a great coach." He winked at La Russo

"Show us how you made that double play last night," said the heavy boy.

"Sure. Third baseman, take the field." Scrapper borrowed a glove and ran out to second. "Now someone hit me a line drive."

It took five pitches before the batter hit one. Scraps gloved it, crossed second, and adding a little showmanship, spun sideways before firing to third.

"Ouch!" The boy covering third took off his glove and shook his hand. "That stung."

"You're not supposed to catch it in the palm of your hand," said Scrapper, laughing.

"Where'd you learn to do that? Twist in the air, I mean," he asked.

"A little trick my dad showed me."

"Your dad? Did he play baseball?"

"Did he play?" asked Scrapper. "You gotta be kiddin'! He was the best first baseman the Phillies ever had."

"It must be great—havin' someone like that around to help you."

*Yeah,* thought Scrapper. *It is great. It just took me a long time to realize* how *great.*

# FOURTEEN

Roberto sat in the Dodger dugout, his foot propped up, and watched his team lose a twilight doubleheader to the Portland Twins. The first game was close, but the second was a blowout. Parsons fell apart in the third inning and the Twins hit everything he threw at them.

*I should have been in there helping*, thought Magic. *Maybe tomorrow*. But when he followed the team inside, he knew it wasn't going to be tomorrow. His toe was still too tender to put his full weight on it. The swelling had gone down but it still hurt.

"Let me see that," said Carter, the Dodgers' trainer, when Roberto took off his socks.

Carter frowned. "Can't tape it," he said. "Wouldn't give you enough freedom to follow through. Are you soaking it like I told you to?"

"Every night," said Roberto. "Warm water and epsom salts."

Something in his voice made Carter look up sharply. "Give it time, Magic. First thing you know you'll be back out on the mound."

Roberto nodded but he wasn't so sure. He'd had a lot of time to think about it. He told himself that he still had a lot to be thankful for. If he never pitched again, he had enough money from his signing bonus to see him through the University of Michigan. He could go ahead with his plans to be a doctor. He hadn't given up on that ambition. But he wanted to play baseball first. More than anything else, he wanted to play baseball.

That night he soaked his toe until it felt comfortable, dried his foot, walked around the small room until he began to stiffen up, and then soaked some more. Gradually, he was able to walk farther and farther. It was only when he tried to twist his body and put all of his weight on his right foot that the pain shot up his leg and his knee buckled.

Still, he kept at it. He had only two days before the game with the Phoenix Giants. Cap had used all the pitchers he had against the Twins. They needed someone fresh.

They needed Magic.

"Think you're ready?" asked Capella when Roberto reported to the clubhouse a few days later.

"Sure." Magic sounded more confident than he felt.

"Good!" The coach clapped Roberto on the shoulder. "I always like to start with the best. Get the jump on them."

As Magic warmed up along the base line he began to relax. Dodger fans soon spotted him and sent up a welcome-back cheer. *This is what it's all about*, thought Roberto, with a rush of gratitude.

But when he got on the mound, he wasn't even aware of the cheers. All he could think about was the man at the plate—a batter who seemed larger than life size. His stomach contracted in a knot of fear.

*Three strikes*, he thought, *that's all I need, three strikes. Then I'll be on my way.* But instead of three strikes, he threw three balls. He knew the batter would take the next one so he tried his split-fingered fastball but when he followed through, his toe gave out on him and he stumbled off the mound as the ball went wide.

Taking off his cap, he walked behind the mound, wiped his brow with his shirtsleeve, and flexed his foot. *Come on*, he thought, looking down at his pitching toe, *give me some help. This is a great way to start a game—walk the first man.*

The second batter counted on Roberto's awkward delivery and let two perfect pitches go by.

*What's with him?* wondered Magic. *Anyone else would have clobbered either of those pitches. They didn't have a thing on them.* He turned the ball over and over in his hand. Then he stretched out and delivered a change-up over the inside corner.

The Giants batter stepped back just enough to lace a hit between the shortstop and third base.

Magic walked the next man to load the bases with no outs. *It's my form*, he thought. *It's all wrong. I'm favoring that toe—gotta forget it.*

*Keep the ball low and inside, not give them anything to lift out.*

He didn't put the ball exactly where he wanted to but the fourth batter hit into a double play and the fifth flied out.

Magic felt as if he'd done a full day's work when he left the mound. His shoulders sagged as he dropped onto the bench. *One more inning like that one,* he thought, *and Cap'll send in a relief. The only thing that saved me was the defense.*

"Lighten up, man," said Graves from his spot beside Roberto. "You can't strike 'em all out. You got lots of help out there."

"Yeah. And I need it." Roberto managed a weak grin.

But he wasn't smiling when the Giants got seven hits and scored two runs in the next four innings, not even after the Dodgers came back with three runs of their own. He struggled with every pitch and each time he ran off the field, he expected to be jerked.

Capella's expression became more and more grim. At the start of the sixth, he sent Parsons to the bullpen to warm up.

*I've got one chance left,* thought Magic, as he faced the first batter of the sixth. *Make it count.* Toeing the rubber, he wound up and fired a fastball to the outside corner. The next few seconds seemed to pass in slow motion. First, the batter leaned back, then he swayed forward, bringing his bat around. There was a loud crack. The ball began to climb. It sailed over the shortstop's head, then over the left fielder's, over the track, and finally, over the fence as the announcer's voice rang out, "Going . . . going . . . gone!"

Roberto swallowed the lump in his throat and looked at Capella. The coach was on his feet, leaning out of the dugout and looking toward the bullpen.

*No*, thought Magic, holding his glove up for a new ball. *I* can *do it.*

He squared his shoulders, glared at the next batter, and fanned him with three perfect pitches. He sent the next two down the same way—nine straight perfect pitches.

Dodger fans exploded. They had their magic man back.

"Wow!" said Graves as he unbuckled his chest protector. "Was that good pitchin' or what!"

"Really grooved 'em in there, my man!"

"Outta sight!"

"Put 'er there!" Stuart held out his hands and Roberto slapped them.

Those three strikeouts gave Magic the confidence he needed. He still had three innings to go—at least nine more batters to face, but he was sure he could do it and when he saw Capella smile, he knew his coach thought so, too.

Only two batters in the remaining innings got a piece of the ball—both for easy outs to first base.

"How's the toe?" asked Carter in the locker room after the Dodgers put away the Giants.

"What toe?" Roberto grinned, stripped, and headed for the showers.

"Ramirez! Hey, Ramirez!" shouted Davidson, Magic's pitching coach.

"He's in the shower," said Graves.

"Well, get him out. Tell him to come to Cap's office on the double. It sounds urgent!"

Roberto clutched a towel around himself and hurried down the concrete hall, leaving wet footprints behind. *Urgent? Something's happened at home. Dad? Mom? Maria, Angelica?* With his heart hammering, he picked up the phone and croaked, "Hello."

He listened for several minutes, uttering an occasional, "Yes." When he hung up, he looked stunned.

"Well?" asked Capella, with a ghost of a smile.

"That was the general manager of the L.A. team," said Magic. "They want me to report in tomorrow." He clutched the edge of the coach's desk as his knees started to give way.

When Magic continued to stand, staring at nothing, Capella asked, "You *are* going, aren't you?"

"Going?" Roberto turned a blank look toward Capella.

"To L.A. . . ."

"Yeah. Yeah! I'm goin'!" Magic's smile lit up his face. *Goin' up,* he thought. *First Scrapper and now me!*

"Well, I think they'd prefer that you arrive in something more than a towel," observed Capella dryly.

Magic looked down at the loosely draped towel and began to laugh. "Yes, sir!" he said, knotting the towel tighter as he ran from the room.


With a half hour to kill at the airport, Magic sat down to watch the evening news on TV but his mind wandered as unfamiliar faces flashed across the screen. Then he saw someone he *did* recognize. Don Sutton, L.A.'s pitcher. He straightened up and listened closely to what Sutton had to say.

"I've had a pretty shaky season," said Sutton to the interviewer. "Up one day and down the next. Those batters look bigger and bigger all the time. When they start hitting my curve ball it's time to hang it up. I'll be forty-two next week, and in baseball, that's old."

"You looked pretty good to me the other night," said the sportscaster.

"Oh, I can still fan a few. It's just a lot harder than it used to be. And I don't want to wait until they knock me all over the ball park. That's why I'm retiring now. Besides, there's a whole new generation of good pitchers out there just waiting for a chance."

"Anyone in particular?"

"Yeah. Roberto Ramirez. If you haven't heard of him yet, you will. He's really hot."

A lump rose in Roberto's throat and he had to look away. Sutton was one of the best, a certain hall-of-famer. His endorsement thrilled Magic but it also gave him goose bumps. What if he failed? What if he didn't live up to Sutton's expectations? To Lasorda's?

There was only one thing for it. He *had* to make good.


When Roberto put on his Dodger blue, white, and red uniform, he wanted to stand before a mirror and admire himself. He didn't, though, because he knew that, as a rookie, he'd be in for enough razzing as it was.

When he ran onto the field at Chavez Ravine, he

was overwhelmed. *This is it*, he thought. *This is where it's* at. And when he took the mound, he marveled at the beauty of the park, at the perfectly manicured grass, and at the ten-inch drop from the rubber to home plate. A pitcher's paradise.

At first he was nervous, with Tommy Lasorda sitting in the dugout watching him with an eagle eye. But after a few pitches, he forgot everything except baseball and the natural high that followed a perfect throw.

He hadn't expected to be a starter right away, and he wasn't. But he did go in as relief pitcher in three games, racking up two wins and one loss.

He did so well that LaSorda told him to rest up—he wanted to use him in the three-game series with the Mets in New York.

*New York*, thought Roberto. *The first thing I'm gonna do is call DT. Maybe we can get together. Boston's not that far.*

# FIFTEEN

With the bases loaded and two outs, David leaned on his bat while a relief pitcher warmed up on the mound. *It's Colson,* he thought. *Throws a mean fastball. Good. The harder it comes in, the faster it goes out.*

"Batter up!" yelled the umpire.

As DT moved in, an organ ground out a familiar tune and Sox fans rose to their feet, crying, "Charge!"

The first pitch, high and outside, was followed by a second blast from the organ and another "Charge!"

*Good time for a hit,* thought David. He backed out of the box and tugged at his gloves. *A single to tie, a double to put us ahead.* Stepping back in, he swung at the next pitch, sending a big rainbow arc over right center. As he ran for first, he saw the Orioles fielder make a gallant effort and crash into the fence as he ran out of real estate. The ball dropped into the stands.

A grand slam! Four RBIs! DT raised both arms to acknowledge the fans' roar and completed the circuit. At home plate he was almost crushed with forearm bashes.

"Al-l-l-l right!"

"*Fantastic!*"

Almost as excited as the players, the fans continued to cheer and applaud for the next three innings, even though there was little action except from the mound, with both pitchers doing their best.

In the middle of the seventh, the organ came to life again with "Take Me Out to the Ball Game" and the fans rose for the seventh inning stretch but no one left his seat. David was coming to bat.

"Charge!"

"Charge!"

DT flexed his knees and straightened up. The first pitch started out high but dropped too soon, for a ball. The second, a wide roundhouse curve, forced him to dodge out of the box.

Behind him, he heard hisses and boos as the Orioles pitcher tried to force him into chopping defensively at the ball with another inside rocket. *The next will be in there*, thought DT. *Do I take it and hope for a walk?*

He stepped out of the box, and using his bat, knocked dirt from his cleats. Then he took some practice swings while he glanced at the third base coach. The man rubbed the back of his neck, took off his cap, resettled the cap, and crossed his arms.

Afraid he had misread the signal, David

switched his gaze to the dugout where Sisko, expressionless, went through the same motions— a green light! Go for it!

DT tapped the plate with the end of his bat.

The Orioles pitcher paused, studied the Sox batter, wound up, and hurled a waist-high fastball.

*That's it*, thought David as the ball sped toward him. Putting all his strength into his swing and breaking his wrists in that microsecond before the bat made contact, he powered one so hard that it was still rising as it cleared the left field fence. No one even made an effort to chase it down. They just stood and watched.

As David rounded second to a deafening roar, his eyes widened in surprise. Sisko was on his feet, leading the rush to home plate, yelling, "A record! A record!" and grinning from ear to ear.

"Let him tag up!" The Sox coach ordered his players away from home plate until David crossed it. Then he let them swamp DT while he stood back and smiled with satisfaction.

"Downtown!" screamed the fans. "Downtown!"

"Downtown, nothin'!" cried Vint over the shouts of his teammates. "That one went into the suburbs!"

David's towering home run took all the fight out of the Orioles, who folded in the eighth and ninth with no runs and no hits.

"That clinches second spot," crowed Valdez in the locker room.

"On to first!" cried Teague, flipping a towel and making it snap like a pistol shot.

"Hey, Green, how far *did* you hit that ball?" asked Whitehall.

"No way to tell." David, excited but also embarrassed by all the attention, shrugged his shoulders.

"Musta been . . ." began Williams, squinting and concentrating, ". . . 400 feet."

"Four hundred? You kiddin'?" scoffed Vint. "That was a rocket, my man—450, if an inch."

"Four-ninety to be exact." Sisko's voice cut through the room, silencing everyone. "Manager of Harry's Pizza just came in. The ball broke one of his windows."

*Uh-oh*, thought David. *Probably one of those big plate glass windows. There goes a week's salary.*

"He wants the ball autographed, Green. Get your clothes on and meet us in my office."

David dressed quickly and hurried down the hall to the coach's room where Sisko introduced him to Harry Wykoff, a grey-haired, medium-sized man clutching a baseball.

"My grandson is gonna love this," said Harry, beaming and handing the ball to David. "He was here today so he saw it go out. Wait'll he comes in the shop to tell me about it and I hand him the ball! Autographed, too! He'll be too excited to sleep for a week."

*So will I*, thought David, trying to keep his hand steady as he wrote on the curved surface. "What about the window?" he asked as he handed the ball back.

"Ah-h-h-h! Don't worry about it. Windows come and go but this . . ." Harry tossed the ball up a couple of feet and caught it as carefully as if it were made of china ". . . this is a once-in-a-lifetime. Young Jory will send you his thanks."

"He'd better send them to Boston," called Sisko as Harry left.

"Boston?" breathed David softly.

"Boston." Sisko smiled and handed David a plane ticket. "It's a commuter flight to New York. The Sox are there now for a three-game series against the Yankees. They need your power."

"But . . ." began David, confused, "how did they know about . . ."

"That record home run?" interrupted Sisko. "They don't. The call up came this morning. I didn't tell you because I didn't want to throw you off your game."

*Boston!* thought David. They wanted *him*. First Scrapper, then Magic, and now *him*. They had all made it to the majors.

"Well, what are you waiting for? Your plane leaves in two hours."

"Yes, sir!" David's voice broke on the "sir," bringing another smile to his coach's face.


David didn't have time to check his luggage through so he had to carry it on board. And when he stepped through the gates of the busy New York terminal, he didn't know which way to go.

*Follow the others*, he thought. He had taken only a few steps when he halted. *Am I hearing things?* he wondered. *Could have sworn someone yelled "DT!" No.* He shook his head and went on.

"Green! Hold up!"

That time he knew he wasn't hearing things— he recognized the voice. "Magic!" he shouted, dropping his suitcases and wheeling around.

Several passengers smiled as the two boys rushed at each other with exclamations, slaps on the back, and punches in the arm.

"Lookin' good, DT!"

"You, too, Magic!"

Roberto picked up one of David's cases. "Come on. We're blocking traffic. Gettin' out of here's a real hassle."

"How'd you know?" asked DT. "That I was comin' in, I mean."

"Hey, this bird knows everything. Why do you think they call me 'Magic'?"

DT laughed. "You sound like Mitchell."

Roberto stopped so suddenly that someone ran into him. "He's got a game tonight. How about you and me watching it on cable tonight?"

"Let's *do* it! Uh . . . after I report in."


That night they watched Scrapper have one of his best games, going three for four and making two spectacular catches. Afterward, they called him.

"Good game, Scraps!" said Roberto.

"Magic! Not doin' so bad yourself, my man. How do you like the Big Apple? Gonna take a bite out of it tomorrow?"

"Yeah. The part they call Shea Stadium."

"There's only one thing wrong with this conversation. It's two-way. Wish we had one of those three-way connections so we could talk to DT, too."

"You got it," said David, leaning closer to the mouthpiece.

"DT?" Scrapper's voice rose to a squeak.

"Yeah, Scraps." David was going to string his friend along but he was too excited. "I made it, too! I am now the Boston Red Sox center fielder!"

"Damn, you know what this means, don't you?" asked an awestruck Scrapper. "We'll be playing against each other for the pennant. And with me on the White Sox, Boston won't have a chance. But . . . that's the way the ball bounces."

DT groaned. "Very funny."

"Hey, you know what else this means?"

"What?" asked Roberto and David in unison.

"It means we beat the odds! Three guys from the same high school make it to the majors at the same time. The odds must be . . ."

"Astronomical!" DT said.

"Yeah. Astronomical. But then . . ." Scrapper's boast came through loud and clear, "*We're* astronomical!"

"Man's got a point," Green said, high-fiving his fellow rookie. "It's the big time from now on—for all of us."

At the close of their first fantastic season as professional ballplayers, all three rookies catch "pennant fever" in the race for the championship in . . .

#5: PLAY-OFF PRESSURE